WILD FRANGIPANI

Katie thinks she's landed a dream job when she travels to the South Pacific island of Naraotoa to manage a hotel. However, her new employer Daniel is an infuriating man who clearly considers her qualifications and experience inadequate. Determined to prove him wrong, Katie settles into her new role, and they even begin to warm to each other — possibly a little too much. For, despite the presence of his gorgeous girlfriend Sharon, Daniel is giving off some extremely flirtatious signals . . .

WENDY KREMER

WILD FRANGIPANI

Complete and Unabridged

LINFORD
Leicester

First published in Great Britain in 2013

First Linford Edition
published 2015

A catalogue record for this book is available
from the British Library.

ISBN 978–1–4448–2298–4

Published by
F. A. Thorpe (Publishing)
Anstey, Leicestershire

Set by Words & Graphics Ltd.
Anstey, Leicestershire
Printed and bound in Great Britain by
T. J. International Ltd., Padstow, Cornwall

This book is printed on acid-free paper

1

Katie took a deep breath in front of the door with the sign stating Private — No Admission. She knocked and entered. Sunlight covered a side-table. It held a silent coffee-machine and neglected thermos jugs. A computer rested amid a shambles of papers and envelopes on the main desk.

He must have heard her. The door opposite opened suddenly. Her new employer's bearing, and his expression, were very confident and assertive. He had an angular, rugged face, with a straight nose, strong chin, and a wide mouth, along with short jet-black hair, tanned skin, and cornflower-blue eyes. He was much younger than she expected. He looked at her, broke into a leisurely smile and held out his hand. It felt pleasant and warm.

'Good morning. You're Katherine Warring? I'm Daniel McCulloch. I hope you had a pleasant journey?'

'Good morning, Mr. McCulloch. Yes, thank you.'

'Please, sit down.' He pointed towards the visitor's chair and sat down behind the desk. 'This is your office; mine is through there.' His eyes skimmed the papers. 'As you see, the mail has piled up. It's mostly advertising stuff and flyers, but there may be enquiries, so check it with care. This hotel isn't my sole concern, but I call to sign papers and give authorization.'

She nodded.

'I'll step up my visits for a while to help you settle in, and you can always contact me by phone in an emergency.'

'Is the work structured in a special way?'

'No, we use the standard hotel software — integrating reservations, keeping up with guest history, front desk information, housekeeping, and so on. If you're dubious about something, just ask and we'll go through it together. Your predecessor adapted the software to fit our own requirements. If you want to improve or change something, I won't object, as long as it benefits the hotel.'

She hoped she sounded casual. 'Do you still have the software manual and details about what your previous manager changed?'

He studied her more carefully. 'Perhaps Marjorie left notes, I don't know. The manual probably disappeared years ago.' He leaned back and played with a pencil. 'I expect you'll soon notice any differences.'

She swallowed hard. There was no point in sidestepping the truth. 'As this is the first time I've been in sole charge of a hotel, help of any kind would be very useful.'

He stiffened. 'What do you mean your first hotel? You're not from the hotel trade?'

Her hands tightened. She cleared her throat. 'I'm a qualified business manager but not expressly in hotel management. I worked in a first-class hotel to finance my studies and know exactly how a hotel functions. I have a business diploma, and worked at management level in a small company. The London agency thought I was suitable.'

Katie recalled that the agency couldn't tell her much about the hotel, or what the job entailed. They probably thought proper hotel qualifications didn't matter if she was going to an island no one had ever heard of. They just wanted managerial qualifications and someone who could get on with people. Katie was confident enough to believe she knew enough about hotel management to handle the job. Excited by the prospect of a job in the South Pacific, she ignored any unease and signed the contract.

For a second Mr. McCulloch scrutinized her silently, and then his irritation began to show.

Slightly harassed, she added quickly, 'I thought they'd cleared my qualifications and everything else with you.'

The pencil snapped in two. Without much consideration in his voice, he said, 'You took a job, knowing you weren't qualified for it? Any fool knows hotel management needs more than clerical skills.'

Katie flinched and coloured.

His index finger hammered the desk. 'The hotel is run from this office and its manager needs skill. If a dim-witted, untrained person makes too many mistakes, it will crash-dive.' His face was grim. 'Perhaps the agency asked the right questions and you kept quiet?'

Out of sight, her hands formed into rounded fists in her lap. How dare he suggest she'd lied to get the job! Katie knew she should avoid an argument, but she wouldn't leave him in any doubt. 'The agency checked my work experience, my qualifications, and references. I did not lie or pretend to be what I'm not.' Her green eyes flashed. 'All I expect is a fair chance and someone I can sound out until I'm established.'

He snapped. 'I don't think you realize how complex this job is. You need to handle furious employees, purchase cleverly, settle disputes with greedy suppliers, calm problematic guests, be at everyone's beck and call, and also run an efficient office.' He leaned back and ran his hands through his thick hair. 'I never spend much time here. I've other businesses to run. Usually I only call to sign papers, or give final authority. You'll need supervising, even if you are some kind of a business manager. Running a hotel is something else!'

Katie longed to retort that any newcomer would need support whether they were qualified, or not. She didn't, because he'd probably silence her with a new barrage of words.

He leaned forward. 'I rely on my manager. I expected disruption, but not a catastrophe.'

Colour flooded her cheeks. Green and blue eyes met silently. She chose her words carefully and tried not to reveal her irritation. 'I'm already very familiar with hotel administration, Mr. McCulloch. Admittedly I'm not a trained hotelier, but I'm not a newcomer either. I can also cope with challenging situations. I've done so plenty of times.' She paused and looked at him without blinking. 'I'm always respectful and courteous too. That comes naturally to me.'

The prospect of handling angry guests or dissatisfied employees worried her, but she wouldn't admit that to him at present. For a moment, she wondered if she ought to pack her bags again and leave, but her determination to prove him wrong choked that idea.

She ploughed on. 'I was truthful. I'm not responsible if the agency handled things wrong. It'll be a complete waste of your money if I leave directly. With your permission, I'll do what I can to keep the wheels turning, until you find someone you think is more suitable.'

He studied her, got up and turned to stare out of the window. His height, the outline of his broad shoulders and slim hips, cast a long shadow across the desk. 'Damn it! Why did I bother about language skills instead of getting someone from New Zealand in the first place?'

He offered no explanation. Katie spoke French quite well and a little German. Perhaps that was why he'd sent his request to the London agency? What an appalling start. 'I'll do my best.'

He turned sharply; his black hair gleamed in the sunlight. 'I don't have much choice, do I?'

She couldn't help baiting him. 'I'm prepared to leave immediately if that's what you want. I won't claim for loss of earnings but I think that my airline ticket plus expenses would be fair, don't you?' She waited, feeling uncomfortable but displaying a bland expression.

He shoved his hands behind his back. Replying brusquely, he retorted, 'Okay! You'll get your chance. Admittedly, I reckoned that handing over would be easy, but clearly it's going to be more time-consuming than I expected. I've an appointment with the bank and I need to organize a machine repair at my plantation. I haven't time to show you much today. I'll come tomorrow, and take you through the basic day-to-day procedures.' He glanced at his watch.

Katie noted the word 'plantation'. She imagined him striding around in jodhpurs, slapping a rawhide whip against his thighs. Although the present circumstances weren't funny, her fantasy escalated and she looked down to hide her amusement. He slapped some keys and a piece of paper down on the desk and Katie flinched.

'I'll have to trust you. Here's the key for the safe, and the computer password. I hope you're computer literate. Do you know how to use Word, Power Point and Excel?'

Katie looked up again without blinking and nodded. She was a qualified commercial manager. Did he think she was brainless? 'Yes.'

'Memorise the password, and then destroy the paper. Don't mess with the programmes. You'll crash the whole system if you experiment. Deal with what you can manage alone. You'll find prototypes of letters in the filing cabinets over there. There's an old-fashioned typewriter in one of the cupboards. I'll check and sign them tomorrow. Tour the hotel, find out where everything is, and absorb as much background information as you can manage.' He sounded more resigned. 'I'll reorganize my schedules and see you tomorrow.' He scribbled on a piece of paper and added it to the other one. 'That's my mobile number, but only in dire emergencies. Ben is the reception manager and on duty today. He knows the hotel like the back of his hand. Ask him if you need information.'

He went to get his briefcase from his office. Leaving, his eyes skimmed down her sleeveless silk top, and along the flow of her trousers until they rested on her feet in their eye-catching sandals.

'Generally, I expect all female members of staff to wear sarongs. I don't expect that of you, but I'd prefer you to wear a skirt or dress and, if possible, modest in style.'

He noted her startled expression. Without waiting for her reply, and with a smile spreading across his face, he covered the distance to the door swiftly and disappeared while still recalling her dazed expression.

2

Katie was furious and fumed inwardly. What a start! Daniel McCulloch was overbearing, and a chauvinistic macho. He hadn't even asked what she was capable of handling, and clearly thought she was an empty-headed bimbo. His remark about what she should wear was old-fashioned, arrogant and sexist.

He hadn't dismissed her outright, but had given her no encouragement either. She'd have liked to throw the job in his face, but then she'd have to pay her own fare home. Once there, she'd be jobless again.

This offer seemed like a wonderful stroke of luck when she saw it in the newspaper. She wasn't sure about that anymore. Slitting the pile of waiting envelopes angrily, she longed to stuff his stupid remarks down his throat and show him she was a first-class manager. If she left, he'd never know just how good she was.

She recalled the journey from London to Naraotoa. At home, it was spring and the gardens were full of daffodils. Here in the South Pacific, it was hot and humid, and flowers bloomed all through the year. She couldn't see much of the exotic scenery on the way from the airport because daylight faded fast in the tropics, but the smell of the South Sea that invaded the taxi's half-open windows was a mixture of sweet-scented blossoms, aromatic shrubs and the salty ocean. It flowed round her face and ruffled her hair. She was tired and euphoric. A job in the South Pacific was a dream come true. When the taxi reached the Rockley hotel, it passed through the wrought-iron gates and sped up a wide tarmac avenue lit by flickering pitch-torches. Their muted glare and spirals of black smoke merged with the night's shadows. The large modern hotel she'd come to manage nestled among tropical gardens.

The receptionist on duty showed her to a neat white bungalow hidden among the gardens at the back of the hotel. One half of it was hers for the duration of her stay. The other half looked silent and unoccupied. He unlocked the door, dumped her two large suitcases inside, switched on the air conditioning, and handed her the keys. 'If you need something, just call the desk. I hope you have a good night's rest.'

Katie gave him a warm smile. 'Thank you. Goodnight!'

After he left, she went back outside onto the small veranda and leaned on the surrounding rail. She could hear the surf breaking onto the sand, and water shimmered through the shadowed greenery. She'd landed in paradise. Her suitcases could wait; the prospect of a walk along the moonlit beach was too enticing. On her return, she had a shower and set her alarm.

This morning she still felt elated as she saw how the sunrise painted the morning in shades of copper and tangerine. Walking through the freshness of the palm-filled gardens, she felt jubilant. She skipped breakfast. She didn't intend to be late when she met her new employer.

Right now, her excitement was fading. She was honest enough to realize her ill-tempered reaction to her new boss was because she was hypersensitive about men in general. She was still infuriated about Paul, and angry at her own stupidity. Usually she remained cool in annoying situations.

Her ex had been good-looking, charming and very appealing. He did everything he could to assure her they were made for each other. He'd met her family once or twice, and her Mum and Dad liked him. Her sister Penny wasn't so convinced. She told Katie to be more critical. In Penny's eyes, Paul was too self-satisfied and too smug. At first Katie didn't take much notice, but her sister's words did have an effect. She'd already noticed Paul was always extremely vivacious in the presence of other girls. He often gave them unnecessary attention and she'd justified his behaviour by telling herself it was his tendency to be

14

over-polite. She told herself no one should be disapproving of someone just because he was courteous and well-mannered. He continued to give her all the attention she hoped for, so it didn't worry her until one evening he suddenly called off their date to go to the cinema. He made an excuse of working overtime. Katie phoned Penny to see if she'd come instead.

Penny had just returned from a shopping expedition and there was a moment of hesitation. She told Katie she'd seen Paul sitting together with another girl in a local restaurant. At first, Katie thought there was a simple explanation. She decided to check for herself. When she arrived, he and the girl were just leaving the restaurant arm in arm. Katie would never forget his blustering explanation or his obvious embarrassment when he saw her. She turned on her heel and never saw him again, even though he phoned several times, trying to talk her round.

She was frustrated about her stupidity, and for trusting him. Penny had seen him for what he was. Why hadn't she? After the first shock faded, Katie realized she hadn't really loved him. Her pride was badly dented and she felt vulnerable, but she didn't miss Paul. Real love went deeper than what she'd felt for Paul. Her feelings were centred on how he'd cheated her, not on the fact that she'd lost him. Soon after, she lost her job when her company went bankrupt. Hitting upon the advertisement for a job in the South Pacific was a fantastic coincidence. It came at exactly the right moment. She applied, got it, and thanked her lucky stars that Paul had shown himself in his true colours when he did.

Tossing her shoulder-length auburn hair, she concentrated on the desk again. It was covered in overtime slips, laundry lists, bills, several booking enquiries, some cheques and advertising junk. She longed to boot the computer but if anything went wrong, Daniel McCulloch would hit the roof. Reluctantly, she decided to wait. She locked any cheques in the safe and went out to reception with some booking enquiries.

Various guests were collecting mail from the reception manager and others were reading newspapers. The lobby was full of over-sized wickerwork chairs flanked by extravagant exotic flowers and plants. She smiled at the desk manager.

He smiled back. 'Welcome to the Rockley. I'm Ben. I hope you'll like it here.'

'Hello Ben. Thanks, I'm Katherine. Katie.'

Ben wore a red and white Hawaiian-style shirt that flowed comfortably over his plump stomach into a pair of smart belted beige slacks.

Katie handed him the papers. 'Can you check these for me, please? Mr. McCulloch wants to go through the computer system with me tomorrow but I think these enquiries need attention as soon as possible.'

'The booking system is simple.' His

fingers flew over the keyboard. 'You just key in, enter the date, and the computer shows what's still available. You book a suitable room if it's free, and mark it with P, for a provisional booking. Then we wait for a confirmation.' Katie looked over his shoulder and nodded. He continued. 'Without the necessary confirmation, we remove it manually or the computer removes it automatically.'

'How long till that happens?'

'Roughly two weeks. We can't block rooms for long; this is a small hotel.'

She nodded. 'Is this the standard programme for bookings, or was it adapted especially for Rockley?'

Ben shrugged. 'I don't know. It's always been the same as far as I know.'

'And the computer information is available to everyone?'

'No. Only to your office and Daniel's. Each department within the hotel is more or less autonomous. We can't access anyone else's.' He turned back to the monitor. 'I'll find provisional booking dates for these.' He glanced at the dates. 'Let's hope we're not too late; the enquiries are days old. Meantime, why don't you introduce yourself to Lesperon, and ask him for office supplies? He's our chef.' He nodded to the left. 'Go down that corridor; the kitchen is first on the left. Lesperon is the loudest guy, making the most palaver.'

Katie paused. Ben clearly knew his way around. If he was prepared to help her, it'd be fantastic. She wanted to avoid asking Daniel whenever possible. 'You've worked here a long time, Ben?'

'Ever since it opened.' He grinned and commented, 'Mr. McCulloch looked a bit hot and bothered just now. Trouble?'

She hooked her hair behind her ears and felt she could trust him. 'I'm not what he expected. I tried to hide my irritation, he didn't.'

Ben laughed and his dark brown eyes twinkled. 'Daniel's bark is worse than his bite. He's used to the hotel running on oiled wheels without much effort on his part. He'll come round.'

She shrugged. 'I hope so. I need

someone to ask when I'm in doubt. Will you help me, Ben? Mr. McCulloch suggested you're the right person to ask.'

'Glad to, if I can.' He grinned and his cheeks bulged like firm apples. 'Don't worry about Daniel. He wants this place to function without a glitch so that he can concentrate on other things. It's his job to explain how. If his routine is upset for a while, that's not your fault. Ask me whatever, and whenever, you like. I'll try to help.'

On the way to the kitchen, Katie was sure that if Ben helped and Daniel McCulloch gave her a fair chance, she'd succeed — and she was determined that she would succeed.

3

Daniel looked in the rear mirror. She certainly was a firebrand, and a very attractive firebrand too. Amusement flickered in his eyes. He started the engine and focused on the road again. His expression steadied. He'd assumed that the hand-over to this new woman would be quick and uncomplicated. Marjorie had run Rockley so efficiently he'd been lulled into a feeling of passive involvement. Her proficiency left him free to manage his other businesses. He'd been grateful because he only needed to sign papers, make critical decisions, and keep a casual check on things. This woman needed backing for a while because if she floundered, the hotel would too, and he wouldn't let that happen. He accelerated, and the silver convertible raced down the empty palm-lined road.

He'd been extremely busy when Marjorie finished and hadn't thought about finding out what she'd changed since she took over. He needed to do so fast. He'd put in a few hours this evening and check through the system before he showed Katie tomorrow.

He tried to remember his exact wording to the London agency. He was sure he must have asked for a professional hotel manager. Why had they chosen her? Left to her own devices, this woman could ruin Rockley, and the thought knotted his stomach. He didn't intend to let that happen. Even if she was a business manager, managing a hotel was a completely different kettle of fish.

He noted unconsciously he was nearing the outskirts of the next small village, and reduced speed. Reluctantly, he admitted it wasn't completely her fault, but the hotel was important, and she wasn't. Regardless of what she thought of him, the hotel was making a steady profit and it must stay that way. He recalled the thick auburn hair, the green eyes fringed with long dark lashes, the smooth English complexion, and her slender figure. She was eye-catching, but that didn't compensate for missing qualifications. She'd concealed her annoyance and stood firm. They were excellent qualities for a manager. His lips twitched. Their meeting was knotty, and if things didn't improve, he'd have to borrow someone from another hotel and spend more time at Rockley himself until he had a proper replacement.

Perhaps he ran too many ventures for his own well-being, but he enjoyed making money and providing jobs for local people. He hated to see the flux of workers to New Zealand and elsewhere. Naraotoa was worth his efforts to keep as many people as he could in employment and on the island. Naraotoa was the greatest place on earth.

A few minutes later he reached Varua, the main town. Brightly painted two-storey buildings bordered the palm-lined main street. Flowering bushes flourished in any gaps and a busy throng of people populated the pavements. He parked the car in a shady spot, waved to an acquaintance, and went through the swing-doors into the small bank. A short time later, he picked up supplies from his warehouse and drove back to the plantation office.

★   ★   ★

Daniel sat alongside her, one arm draped along the back of her chair. For some reason he enjoyed the chance to study her close up. Her perfume was light and suited her very well. He remarked, 'You've marked the third and fourth entries as bookings but the third one is a provisional booking. I expect you entered the wrong code number?' She hadn't completely adjusted to his company yet but she accepted his directives without any comments or arguments. She was clearly getting used to his daily visits and the atmosphere in the office had improved a little. It wasn't as cordial as he hoped for but it was okay.

To his surprise, guiding her through the pitfalls had been easier than he expected. He could already leave her to cope with the daily business because she did have a very good insight into hotel management. He decided not to mention her contract again. Why should he? It was counter-productive to remind her of their first meeting. A contract was a contract. He hadn't cancelled it and she was still here. He was satisfied with her progress and it looked like things would work out after all.

Katie concentrated on the monitor. She ruffled through her notebook for the right page and after checking, she said, 'You're right. The provisional code is thirty-four and the confirmation code is thirty-five.'

'Okay, correct it.' He got up and picked up a pile of papers lodged on his side of the desk. 'Here, these are okay.' He handed her the bundle. 'Oh, I talked to Mrs. Hicks on the way in; she mentioned she needs replacements for next week's duty rota. Fixed that yet?'

'Almost. She also needs a replacement cleaner tomorrow. I'll sort that out this morning.'

He nodded and moved smoothly towards his office door, commenting as he went. 'Okay, but do it right away. Always give personnel problems priority. If the day-to-day services don't function properly, you'll soon be up to your neck in hot water.'

She looked down pointedly at the work on her desk and replied, 'It gets priority over everything else?'

He stuck his head back round the door, and in a relaxed manner, he smiled. 'Organising one replacement will take you all of five minutes. Is next week's duty rota ready? They'll need some extra waiters for that celebration on Tuesday evening.'

'Yes, I know. I've already accounted for that.'

He moved past her desk towards the door with his briefcase tucked under his arm. 'Once you've sorted that out, finish off those overtime entries. The bank needs the wage list by Friday, so wrap it up this afternoon too. I'll check it tomorrow.'

Katie nodded.

'By the way, fire that waitress. Today or tomorrow.' He looked at her enigmatically, and saw what he expected. 'You're uncomfortable with it, aren't you?'

She felt flustered and admitted, 'I've never had to dismiss anyone before. I'm not sure how.'

He ran his hand down his face. 'Okay! Leave it up to me. Order her to the office tomorrow morning. I'll do it. You can see how I handle it. It's best to remain curt and objective. Give explanations whenever necessary and then just hand them their papers. Don't tie yourself up in words of regret or sympathy. That makes it worse for you and for them. Next time you'll manage it on your own. It happens more often than you think. There's always a lot of comings and goings in hotels, especially in the less-skilled jobs.'

Her face brightened and his expression relaxed into a smile. 'Thanks!' she said.

He waved his hand in a gesture of dismissal and vanished from sight.

She admired the way he handled the interview with the waitress next day. He was firm without sounding cruel. The girl had been caught stealing hotel property. Daniel coped with her halting protests and silenced her with a few words, quoting the evidence of fellow workers who'd seen her stuffing things into her bag. She grew silent and looked at him petulantly before she snatched the papers and left.

Daniel watched her close the door. 'Silly woman! As if it's worth losing your job for the sake of some towels and some shampoo. She can't apply to us for a reference, because she knows it would be a bad one, and her chances of finding a decent job on Naraotoa again are next to zero.'

4

After he left, Katie realized she felt happier with each passing day. She leaned back, straightened her skirt, and busied herself with the remaining entries. She got up to fill her mug with coffee and watched his car speeding down the driveway. His detached, competent, and focused attitude in the office couldn't quite stifle the red-blooded, magnetic quality he had. She had to admit he wasn't just intelligent, but he was good looking and sexy too. She wasn't blind to his attractions. He presented a friendly, communicative face to her and the rest of the world but she sensed that he had also a private side to his character that he guarded closely.

Female guests and hotel employees eyed him with special interest, even though he made no obvious effort to attract anyone. She wondered if he ever picked up girlfriends in the hotel. Although the staff revelled in gossiping about him, they'd never said so. If that was the case, it was good. When an owner got too involved with guests, or had an affair with an employee, it caused trouble. It was better if he restricted his hunting grounds to other places. She was glad he didn't interest her — she'd had enough of men for a while.

Katie telephoned and organized a replacement cleaner and then went to give the housekeeper the details and the duty rota for the following week.

Mrs. Hicks smiled. 'Good! Now I can tell Ruby she can have next Wednesday off. She wants to be sure that she can go to a birthday party on an outlying island. There have been a lot of delays to the boat services recently and she wanted to be sure she had enough time to get there and back in time.'

'What's the trouble? Is it unusual for the boats to be late? Is there something

30

special going on?'

'We're not really sure. According to Ruby, the police have been making regular spot checks recently and that holds everything up. They're checking luggage and all sorts of things.'

'What are they looking for?'

'Who knows! Things that people smuggle I expect. Everything is so expensive in the shops. No one asks where items come from, if they can get them cheaper. Apparently, the police are also asking too many questions about everyone and everything. It's making people nervous. No one under-stands why, and they don't give any explanations.'

'Not popular, I'm sure, but they have to do their job. There's probably a good reason.'

Mrs. Hicks tilted her head. 'Everyone knows the policemen personally. Apart from the senior officer, they're all local men. People would stop buying and concealing forbidden goods for a while if that's the reason and it would stop all these unnecessary delays.'

Katie laughed. 'Sounds like a film script to me.' She liked the jovial housekeeper. She'd already shared some tea-breaks with her, and she wished she could stop for a chat now, but Daniel's tasks beckoned.

A slim, attractive woman with delicate features, curly blond hair and friendly grey eyes stood chatting to Ben near the reception desk.

'Katie, this is Mrs. Stannard. She wanted to speak to Daniel, but I explained he's left.'

She smiled. 'Yes, that's right. Hello! I'm Katherine Warring. Katie. Mr. McCulloch left half an hour ago.'

'Hi, I'm Laura.' She frowned. 'Pity! I was passing and thought I'd catch him here. I was hoping for a donation towards sports equipment for the youth club. It doesn't matter; we'll see him soon anyway.'

'I'll tell him you called. Can I offer you something to drink?'

Laura broke into a leisurely smile.

'What a good idea. Thank you!' She followed Katie into the office.

Laura accepted the glass of cold pineapple juice and hung a roomy raffia shoulder bag over the chair. 'So, you're the new manager? Do you like it here? Rockley isn't the snazziest hotel on the island, but it's first-rate, very popular, and it's always busy.'

'I love it. I'll like it even more when I'm truly in command.' She noted Laura's puzzled expression. 'I've never officially worked as hotel manager before. I still have a lot to learn, but I'm enjoying it very much.'

Laura studied the younger woman's friendly face. 'Oh, I see! David and I come here for a meal occasionally. We prefer Rockley to the two bigger hotels on the other side of the island. They're pricey and very grand. Been there yet?'

'No, but I've heard about them. I haven't explored the island properly yet, but I will as soon as things are running smoothly.' Katie asked casually, 'Do you know Mr. McCulloch well?'

Laura nodded. 'We're friends.'

'Does your husband own a business of some kind, or is he a government official?'

Laura chuckled softly. 'Heaven forbid! David's a doctor. He came as a fill-in when a previous doctor at the hospital retired. No one else applied and by then we were hooked on the island. Do you like Naraotoa?'

'It's wonderful; I love it.' Her eyes sparkled as she leaned forward to refill Laura's glass.

'I'm glad. Some people enjoy it for a while because they feel they're on a kind of holiday, but that soon wears off and most people begin to get bored. Technical progress here is slow, and islanders are interested in things that people elsewhere aren't.'

'I don't think I'll get bored. I love the unspoiled beaches and the friendly people. I wouldn't change a thing.'

Laura looked at her watch. 'Oh, heavens! I'm late for a get-together, but I'm glad that we've met, Katie. Come and visit me one day.'

'I'd like that very much.'

Laura hoisted her bag and smiled contentedly at her before she nodded and left.

5

Next morning, Katie waited apprehensively for Daniel's appearance. She'd been entering information yesterday afternoon when the computer crashed. She'd tried solving it herself, without success. Her usual method of simply re-starting the whole system, at the risk of losing what she'd just added, hadn't worked either.

He breezed in and saw from her expression that something was wrong. Dumping his case on the side table, he said. 'What's up? You look like you've just seen a ghost. Has our venerated chef thrown one of his tantrums again?'

'No, I can handle Lesperon most of the time.' Katie explained what had happened. 'I've tried to sort it out on my own, without success.'

Without commenting, he sat down behind her desk. 'I presume you've tried re-starting?'

'Of course. Several times! It didn't work.'

He rubbed the back of his hand across his mouth and then reached forward to disconnect the computer completely from the power supply. 'Let's try starving it of food for a while, and see what happens.' He noticed her anxious look. 'Katie, don't worry! You know that the computer automatically backs up the main system from time to time, as well as the programmes you were using before it went haywire. The most annoying thing that could happen is that you've lost the work you were doing when it occurred. If we can't solve it ourselves, I'll ring Harvey Winters — he's a whiz at showing computers who's boss. Let's have a cup of coffee and go through any hitches you've noticed since yesterday'

'I always try to be careful. I don't know what happened or why.'

He nodded. 'Don't worry! It is not the end of the world. You probably used a combination of two keys that sent it skew-whiff. It's happened to me a couple of times.'

After they'd settled some of the other work, he reconnected the main cable a couple of minutes later and pressed the start button. Katie heard the familiar bonging sound and knew that the problem was solved. They discovered that various entries from her previous afternoon's work were missing, but everything else looked intact and unharmed.

He got up. 'You'd better check through everything you entered from about lunchtime yesterday, or at least just before it collapsed on you.' He rose and picked up his case.

Smiling with relief, Katie said, 'Thanks! I could kiss you for sorting it out so fast!'

Daniel tilted his head to the side and with a bland half-smile said, 'That's an offer that's hard to resist, but I'll stand firm this time.'

Katie was momentarily lost for

words, but he turned away and went into his room.

* * *

Although Daniel continued to keep up the pressure, Katie's confidence grew with every passing day. After working hours, she now enjoyed exploring the island properly. She borrowed a hotel bike and cycled along the island's coastal road with the bluish-turquoise ocean on one side, and pineapple, banana, papaya and citrus plantations on the other. She passed shanty sheds selling fruit juice, fruit and vegetables. The owners always had a smile and a cheerful word. Varua, on the other side of the island, was Naraotoa's only real town. Katie still thanked heaven that fate had brought her to the island.

She decided to revive a neglected hobby. She'd always enjoyed sketching and painting during her school days, but it had faded into insignificance as she grew up. Naraotoa was a perfect place to resume her interest. There was endless beauty in the flowers and scenery. Her pleasure in trying to capture what she saw returned, despite the fact that the resulting pictures were far from professional. One day, a maid sidled up the veranda steps to see what she was doing and she spread the word that their manageress was an artist. Katie knew she was only mediocre and didn't enjoy the ensuing curiosity until she realized it gave her a chance to empathise with workers she'd otherwise seldom see.

Every Friday evening during the high season, the hotel put on an Island Night of Polynesian Dancing and Music, together with local food and drink. Katie sat in the shadows and watched. Talking to Ben about it next day, she told him how much she'd enjoyed it.

Ben nodded. 'It's part of our cultural heritage. These days commercial entertainment has changed everything, but dancing is still important to us. Perhaps it would even die out completely without tourism.'

Laura phoned one morning. 'Katie? Remember me — Laura?'

'Yes, of course. Nice to hear from you.'

'How about visiting me one after-noon?'

'I'd love to.'

'Good. How about Tuesday?'

'Where do I find you?'

6

Daniel didn't need to spend much time at Rockley any more. The business of showing Katie the ropes had gone well. Once or twice, he thought about reassuring her about her contract but then decided to avoid rubbing salt into the wound. Why remind her of their first interview? He liked a good-humoured atmosphere in the office and even though things were more relaxed, Katie remained wary and distant. If she still remembered her thorny welcome, it was no wonder that she remained cautious and reserved.

He'd almost put it out of his mind, until one day while making his rounds to check on appearances and the atmosphere of the place, Daniel met Katie, with the housekeeper and a room-cleaner, in one of the corridors. They were laughing about something.

Suddenly he realized that Katie never laughed much in his company. She was friendly but not carefree, and that bothered him. Generally, he won women over easily with words and a little charm. Katie's restraint goaded him. He told himself it was silly for him to bother about something so unimportant.

*　*　*

After going on a cruise with Daniel in his yacht one afternoon, David persuaded him to come back to the bungalow for some of Laura's cake and iced coffee.

They all discussed local happenings for a while, then Laura remarked, 'I met your new manager recently.'

Daniel nodded. 'Yes, she told me. You came for money again!'

'Yes, and I haven't forgotten.'

Daniel sighed. 'Okay! I'll write you a cheque before I leave.'

'Good. We need basketballs and new cricket nets, so be generous.' She took a sip from her glass. 'She's a very nice girl.'

'Who?'

'Katie. I was surprised to hear she isn't a trained manager. Did you know that beforehand?'

Warning lights flashed in his brain. Laura was rarely interested in the hotel. 'No, but she's coping okay so far.'

'You didn't know she wasn't a professional?'

He paused. 'No I trusted the agency to choose someone suitable. I wasn't overjoyed when she arrived. But it's working out better than I expected.'

'She still needs lots of backing to cope with the hotel single-handed though.'

Daniel edged forward and took a piece of coconut cake. 'Hey, this looks good.' He didn't want to discuss Katie. He took a generous bite. 'Absolutely yummy, Laura. Nothing beats home cooking.'

'Then get married.'

He smiled. 'All the best women are taken.'

'Nonsense! You keep repeating your-self! You're too popular; otherwise

44

you'd try harder to find someone.'

He grimaced. 'Why choose one pineapple when there's a basketful on offer for the same price?'

'Because one perfect pineapple tastes better than a lot of motley ones.'

Daniel could tell she was off on her favourite hobby horse again. He appealed silently to David.

David hurried to oblige 'Have you heard that Eddie's bought a new set of sails? They must have cost him a bomb.'

Daniel was grateful for the change in the conversation. He didn't want to talk about his private life or about Katie anymore!

7

Katie found Laura's home easily. It overlooked the town, on the outskirts of Varua. Several flame-trees coloured the garden and purple bougainvillea formed a generous hedge along the fence. Glancing across, as she approached the bungalow, there was riotous colour from local exotic flowers flourishing on the edges of the patch of wiry grass.

Laura came out to greet her. 'Hello! I saw you coming up the road.'

Katie climbed the steps and Laura gestured towards some thick-cushioned bamboo chairs on the veranda. Looking back down towards the town and the small harbour, Katie murmured, 'What a fabulous view.'

'I'm almost ashamed to say I take it for granted these days, but I agree that the colours everywhere on the island are terrific, aren't they?'

'Yes spectacular, especially the plants. You'd have to pay a fortune in Europe for flowers that grow here like weeds!'

'If you like impressive views, Daniel has some, up and down the coastline in both directions from his bungalow. Perhaps you'll see them one day. Like some coffee or fruit juice?'

'Coffee, if it's no trouble.'

'Coming up!'

The sun was weakening and breezes ruffled the plants in the garden and in the large terracotta tubs lining the veranda. Laura returned with a loaded tray.

'Do you work, Laura?' Katie asked her.

'No, well, not for money. There's no financial demand for me to work. I do voluntary work at the hospital and help run the youth centre. There's not much employment for women on Naraotoa anyway, but I don't miss a regular job.'

'Children?'

'Just one. Ian. He's starting university and is in Christchurch looking for digs

47

at present.' She looked into the distance and her voice sounded very wistful.

'He'll be all right, I'm sure. Teenagers are very independent these days; although I expect it's never easy to let go, is it?'

Laura looked at Katie. 'I knew I'd miss him, but not so much. He's very sensible and outgoing and I'm sure he'll enjoy university. I just haven't got used to the idea that he doesn't need us anymore and that he's leading his own life.' She paused. 'You must think I'm very silly to prattle on about him like this.'

'No, of course not. I think I understand, but you want him to spread his wings, don't you?'

'Yes, of course. It's just because he was the centre of our lives, and he's left a gap.'

Katie wanted to divert her thoughts. 'Then you'll have to fill the gap somehow. More voluntary work perhaps?' She paused and hoped Laura could help. 'Do you know of someone who'll give me golf lessons, Laura? I'd like to try, but not with a professional instructor, in case I hate it.'

Laura poured coffee and looked intrigued. 'Golf? Actually, I play golf. Not very well, but probably enough to help start a beginner.' Katie noticed how the idea had already caught her imagination.

'You'd like a go?'

Katie nodded eagerly.

'I used to play regularly with a friend of mine, but she developed chronic back pain so I gave it up too. Rockley's golf course is busy mornings, but it's often empty late afternoon. We could use that and you could borrow hotel clubs for free.'

'I wouldn't want to do that. I'd be setting a bad example. Do you have time and enough patience to cope with a beginner? If so, I finish about four every day.'

'What about next Thursday afternoon?'

'Yes, perfect!' Katie looked around. 'I like your bungalow. It's very attractive.'

Laura nodded. 'We bought it from David's predecessor and we're very happy here. In an emergency, David can walk to the hospital.' She paused. 'I was wondering where you saw the advert for your job.'

'In a national paper. Everyone dreams of the South Pacific. I expect the agency had dozens of applications. I'll never know why I got it, but I presume it was because I could leave immediately. I'd lost my previous job and also just split up from my boyfriend. There was nothing to stop me.'

'It was still plucky to come without knowing what to expect. Your boyfriend, was he someone special?'

Katie shrugged. 'I thought so when we first met. We went out for several weeks. Then I discovered him messing round with someone else. I was shocked at the time but now I'm glad it happened. I know now that I didn't love him. I lost my job and saw the advert for a manager for the Rockley. I'd nothing to lose, and applied.'

'Quite honestly, when we first met I wondered if you'd live to tell the tale, because your predecessor was very efficient. She set high standards. Weren't you worried?'

Katie laughed weakly. 'Not until I met Mr. McCulloch. I didn't know much about the job until I got here. The agency in London thought I was perfectly suitable. I now realise that they didn't understand the complexities. Running an office is easy, but a hotel is a lot more complicated. I still struggle now and then, but Ben is a wonderful support and I'm improving every day.'

Laura pushed a strand of hair out of her face. 'It'll get easier in time. Do you get on with Daniel?'

Katie shrugged and cleared her throat. 'Generally, yes. We had a bumpy beginning but he's been surprisingly patient. We manage quite well.' Katie hoped Laura didn't probe too much. She hadn't made up her mind about Daniel herself yet.

'David will be home soon. Stay and share our meal.'

'Thanks; that's kind of you. I'd like that very much.'

8

'Daniel's unusual, isn't he? It's not surprising that women are interested in him.'

Katie sipped her coffee. 'I'm not sure if the word 'unusual' is right. I do know that he gets his way without people noticing he's manipulated them, and he's clever. He also attracts women without much effort.'

Laura's eyebrows arched and lifted. 'He's an eligible bachelor and that makes him a target for busy tongues and hopeful girls.'

Katie smiled and her eyes twinkled mischievously. 'I know I shouldn't listen, but the hotel workers gossip about him incessantly. His lifestyle fascinates them. The women want someone to trap him and the men don't understand how he manages to stay single. Do you know what annoys me most? Everyone thinks

I've landed the best job on this planet.'

Laura chuckled. 'Do they?'

Katie nodded. 'They even tell me so. They should try it! They'd soon change their minds. Daniel is a workaholic but I don't mind that. He also knows how to make money, and I suppose he deserves it. He works hard. Can I help you with the meal?'

Laura looked at her watch briefly and picked up the tray. 'Follow me!' She gathered the various utensils from the cupboards and drawers. Getting some cold chicken from the fridge, she said, 'Here, cut this up into pieces. I hope he doesn't end up as an eternal bachelor. He likes children. He'd make a good father, and a good husband.' She noticed Katie's raised eyebrows and sceptical expression. 'No, honestly, I mean that. I've known him a long time.'

The two women were still busy chatting when they heard steps on the veranda.

'Oh, David, that's good. He's punctual for once.'

Laura's husband sauntered in and kissed her. 'Hello, my love.' He gave Katie a warm smile. He was tall and slender with friendly features. 'And you must be Katie? I know all about the good-looking green-eyed manageress at the Rockley. Don't ask me how.' He viewed their efforts. 'What a picture of domesticated bliss — two women preparing food for a famished male. Yummy!'

'Don't get carried away, Dave. You'll be helping with the washing-up later. We're nearly ready. Take Katie out onto the veranda and give her something to drink. Take the plates and the cutlery, Katie, and I'll bring the rest.'

'Your wish is my command, my darling.' David made a sweeping gesture. 'Come with me, Katie. We'll enjoy some wine I've stashed away for special occasions.'

Katie picked up the plates and followed him. While he organised the wine in the living room she arranged the plates and cutlery, and then sank into one of the veranda chairs. He came out and handed Katie her glass and went to give Laura hers.

Katie rotated the pale liquid and took a sip. It tasted fine. Daylight had almost faded, and haunting birdsong echoed throughout the garden. When David returned, she asked him, 'How big is the hospital? Laura pointed where it is from here, but I didn't notice it. I must have passed it on my way up.'

'It's partly hidden from the road. There's a big sign, but you must have looked ahead and missed it. The clinic isn't very big — three wards, some treatment rooms and an operating theatre. But we handle everything from in-growing toenails to a Caesarean.'

'How many doctors are there?'

'Three. It houses the island dentist too. It's easier for everyone if all the medical facilities are together. If we get a patient who needs treatment beyond our capabilities, we helicopter them out to Auckland.'

'It seems a lot of doctors for an island this size.'

'Ah well, we're family and hospital doctors. We cover the five outlying islands too. We go to them, if they can't come to us.'

'Do you like being a doctor?'

'Yes. I don't think you should be a doctor unless you're dedicated to the idea. My dad was one too, for almost fifty years. I still face most of the illnesses he did, but immunisation and medication have improved things. Luckily, family bonds on Naraotoa are still strong, and that helps if some of the problems aren't just physical ones.'

Katie listened and sipped her wine.

'We warn kids about drug abuse, about too little or too much food, and we hope we're planting some seeds of wisdom.' He shrugged. 'It's all part of the job. Laura was a nurse. That's why she copes so well with my work.'

'Really? I didn't know she's an ex-nurse. How long have you lived here?'

'Thirteen . . . no, it's fifteen years now. We arrived on Ian's fourth birthday.'

'Laura loves it here, doesn't she?'

'Yes, otherwise I'm sure she'd pressure me to move. I'm glad you're friends. Ian's departure has left her down in the dumps.'

Katie nodded but added no comment. The wine slipped down her throat and left a pleasant taste on her tongue.

'She probably delights in having someone else to worry about. She misses Ian dreadfully and I think you'll help cheer her up no end.'

'I'm glad we met. I like her. I haven't met many people yet.'

'You'll soon make friends. People are friendly; they don't generally get off on the wrong foot like Daniel did.'

Katie looked up in surprise. 'How do you know that? Did he say something?'

'Not in so many words, but he made some remarks and I drew my own conclusions. Laura thinks he did a clog dance when you arrived. He gets on well with her, but has to fight for his privacy. Laura knows it's none of her business, but she doesn't stop trying to marry him off.'

Katie chuckled.

David stretched his legs. 'She won't make the slightest difference. He'll leave us all standing when he leads the right woman down the aisle.'

The meal was spicy chicken with noodles and a creamy pudding for desert. Tiny insects buzzed around the candle. They burnt with a hiss when they touched the flame.

Katie could tell that Laura and David were still in love. They interlinked their conversation and kept constant eye contact. David's job and Laura's concern for others kept them on parallel wavelengths. David was the practical one, and Laura's quixotic and inquisitive mind balanced their relationship perfectly.

They were both nice people and generous hosts. Katie hoped they could help her solve a dilemma. The hotel was functioning quite well now, and Ben had supported her all the way. Katie wanted to say thanks. 'Do you know Ben, the reception manager at Rockley?'

Laura nodded. 'Of course. Everyone knows Ben.'

'He's helped me no end and I want to say thank you, but I wonder if it's okay. I don't want to give his wife the wrong impression.'

The Stannards laughed and David said, 'Don't measure things by European standards. Giving is part of the lifestyle here. His wife won't mind, but give him something that won't disappear with the first visitor who says they fancy it.'

Laura added, 'Give him some packs of beer, or a bottle of pineapple liquor. At least he'll get some of that. I'll get a bottle direct from the distillery here in town if you like, and bring it on Thursday. It's cheaper than buying it in the store.'

Katie nodded gladly. They chatted a while and David told them one of the island's policemen had been admitted that afternoon with a gunshot wound.

Laura said, 'Good Heavens! What happened?'

He shrugged. 'It looks like someone had it in for him; someone was lying in wait. He didn't see who it was. Luckily, it wasn't a serious injury. It was a clean shot through his upper arm.'

'How awful!' Katie glanced at her watch. 'Gosh, the time has flown! Thanks for a lovely meal. I'll see you on Thursday, Laura?'

'Yes. The bus service is too irregular in the evening. Take a taxi. They're not expensive.'

'I thought I could walk home across the island.'

Laura chuckled. 'It's too late to even try. Anyway, there's a lot of uphill and downhill, no real path and plenty of tropical undergrowth blocking the way. Even with a good sense of direction, it's further than you think. There's been talk about making a road from one side to the other for years but people don't really want it. It might spoil the island. I'll phone for a taxi; a company that Daniel's in partnership with.'

Katie's face mirrored her surprise. 'Good heavens. What else does he own?'

Laura punched the number. 'The plantation, a grocery store, Rockley, a partnership in a deep-sea fishing company, and this taxi company. Don't judge Daniel too hastily. He's not just a money-making machine. He's very generous. He gives sailing courses at the youth club, donates more than anyone else I know to social causes, and he supports people financially when they start businesses. He isn't as mercenary as you seem to think.'

Katie looked towards the garden blanketed in shadows but didn't comment. Laura and David told her about Varua, and the names of some of the plants in the garden, until the taxi arrived.

9

Laura drove to meet Katie in her husband's Japanese car. She parked it in a shady spot and met Katie on the terrace for a drink. Katie fetched them some bright green cocktails.

'Tried snorkelling yet?' Laura asked. She sucked the liquid through the straw, and chewed on a decorative slice of mango.

'I listened to someone explaining how to do it, to some visiting children, but I expect it's more difficult than it sounds.'

'If you're nervous, I'll come with you. It's the only way to enjoy the coral reefs. Once you get the knack, you'll love it. I don't go scuba diving anymore, but snorkelling is fun.'

Katie laughed. 'Why don't you and David move in here for a while? Golf! Snorkelling! Anything else I should try?'

'Oh, there's deep-sea fishing, sailing, surfing, water skiing, jet skiing, kayaking, Hoby Cats, and lots of land-based sports like tennis, croquet, beach volleyball, zip-lining, and so on.'

Katie lifted her hand in silent protest. 'Hang on before I fall over from sheer exhaustion just thinking about all of that. What's zip-lining?'

Laura chuckled. 'They've only erected one recently. As far as I understand, you fly through the trees on zip lines from the highest point of the island almost down to the beach near Crooked Cove. I'm going to give it a try one day.'

Katie laughed. 'It sounds fun. I'll come with you.'

Laura pointed to Katie's hat. 'That's pretty, but not practical.'

'Okay. I'll leave it with the barkeeper.' The crushed remains of Laura's drink plummeted to the bottom. 'I'm ready. What about you?'

They made their way to the golf course with its wiry grass. Laura showed Katie how to stand, how to grip the club, and how to swing it. Katie tried to copy.

Daniel's car cruised up the driveway and Laura noticed it. He seldom came at this time of day. Katie assumed he was making one of his spot-checks again. Laura waved her club and shouted. Katie glanced, clenched her teeth and hoped he'd go away. He didn't. He came towards them wearing a sky-blue shirt that mirrored his eyes, and beige slacks that glided smoothly over slim hips.

Laura greeted him with easy familiarity. 'Hi, Daniel.'

He removed his sunglasses. 'Hi! What's this about?'

'I'm teaching Katie how to play golf.'

Katie tucked a strand of hair behind her ear and felt obliged to comment. 'It's not easy, is it? I keep missing. Even if I do manage to hit the ball, it always lands off target.'

'How about giving her some tips, Daniel?'

Nervously, Katie hurried to sidetrack the suggestion. 'Oh, don't trouble Mr. McCulloch.'

Laura chuckled. 'You're both off duty now. Do you two need an introduction? Daniel, this is Katie; Katie, this is Daniel.'

The laughter lines at the corners of Daniel's eyes deepened.

Katie had made up her mind to keep her distance from him socially, if she could. When she looked at him now, she had to admit he was a very attractive man, but she shelved the thought hastily.

His eyes narrowed and his expression was bland when he said. 'If you pick up golf as fast as your job, you'll soon be Naraotoa's title holder. What you actually need is lessons from a qualified instructor. I'm an amateur.'

Unable to avoid his glance, the colour covered her cheeks. It was silly to let him unsettle her like this. His voice was as friendly as ever, but she was on her guard. She'd had enough of men she couldn't trust, and Daniel already had a reputation. 'I'm not very ambitious. I don't want to bother with a qualified instructor. I'm quite happy enjoying myself with Laura's help.'

'Well you won't enjoy anything much if you never hit the ball.'

She capitulated. 'Okay! Can you tell what's wrong?'

'I wasn't watching. Show me.'

She concentrated. Remembering Laura's instructions, she swung and missed pathetically.

He moved behind her. His breath on her neck and his physical nearness made her incredibly nervous. Encompassed within the curve of his muscular arms, he re-positioned her hand. 'Keep your grip there and focus on the target. Swing back and hook the club behind your head and follow through like this.' Katie had never experienced such a strong physical reaction to any man before. How ridiculous!

She looked up. Brilliant blue eyes met speckled ones. For a moment, Katie was mesmerised by his nearness and the tangy sandalwood smell of his skin. No wonder women fell for him.

The top of her head barely reached his chin; her burnished hair brushed his chest. He made another practice swing with her, and then stepped aside to watch.

Freed from his presence, Katie steadied her balance and kept her grip where he'd put it. She took a swing. The club hammered into the ball, which flew through the air. It landed wide of its target, but at least she'd made contact. She felt quite elated.

'Good!' Laura clapped her hands.

Katie smiled and looked at Daniel. 'What a difference. Thank you!'

A fleeting emotion travelled across his face. 'I'd still invest some time and money in professional help if I were you. You'll enjoy yourself much more. Not that I'm carping about Laura's help, of course, but a professional trainer is just that — a professional.' He looked at his watch. 'Anything unusual, office-wise?'

Back on safer ground, Katie answered, 'Nothing special. Lesperon has requested replacement china for the restaurant. Will you check it, please — in case he's over the top again?'

He gave them a good humoured smile and a ghost of a nod before he turned away and went towards the entrance.

Katie concentrated on golf. Thoughts continued to unsettle her. Daniel's magnetic personality was part of his genetic makeup. Some men were sexy without any effort on their part. She wasn't interested in his company, but she was pleased to hear him admit that she was managing her job. She ignored further reflections and paid attention to Laura instead.

10

By the following Thursday, Katie's ability had improved slightly, even if she still missed the shot now and then. At the moment it was Laura's turn, and she whacked the ball with practised ease.

'Have you heard about Daniel's new girlfriend?'

'No, we don't exchange much personal information.' Katie didn't add that she deliberately avoided being too inquisitive. They had a friendly working relationship and that was enough.

'She's a receptionist called Sharon. She works in one of the other hotels.'

Katie mused that nothing stayed secret for long on an island only thirty miles in circumference. Laura picked up gossip like a jackdaw gathering silver. The name jogged Katie's memory; someone called Sharon had phoned him several times recently. She didn't mention that to Laura. Single men, or women, didn't have an easy life on Naraotoa.

Laura continued, 'She's very attractive — blonde, tall, well dressed, outgoing, and a good sportswoman. She's from New Zealand; hasn't been here very long. I met her recently. She's a very boisterous character.' Laura asked, 'What about you? Met anyone interesting yet?'

'No, and I don't need anyone. I'm still regretting my last mistake.'

'I hope you don't intend to ignore men indefinitely? That'd be a terrible waste of time.'

Katie laughed. 'You're incorrigible!'

★　★　★

Next morning, she handed Ben the bottle of liquor Laura had got for her. 'Thanks a million for all the help and support,' she said.

His shiny cheeks bulged, and his dark chocolate eyes sparkled. He brushed his brilliant Hawaiian shirt with his large hands and accepted the bottle with embarrassment. 'It was my pleasure. I was happy to help now and then. This isn't necessary.'

'You saved my bacon very often. I want you to know I realize that.'

* * *

In the office, the atmosphere improved noticeably. She handled the routine work with confidence and her knowledge about the hotel's workings grew daily. Daniel could now fully concentrate on his other undertakings again like he'd done before.

* * *

One afternoon Ben stopped Katie as she left the office. 'Would you like to come to my village on Sunday? It's a special occasion, a religious celebration. Come and meet my wife and my family.'

Her smile was eager with delight. 'I'd love to. Where? What time?'

'Late afternoon. It's easy to find us; we're the first village on the beach after you pass the church.'

11

On Sunday, the orange and gold sun blazed down all day as Katie lazed in the shade and read a paperback. When the sky changed to shades of fuchsia and lilac, she went to shower and change into a casual top and matching skirt.

The beach was almost deserted when she set out for Ben's village. The sea was boisterous and waves crashed noisily on the sand. The wind messed her hair thoroughly before she'd gone a dozen steps. She found Ben's village easily, and followed a well-trodden path from the crest of the beach through the greenery. She arrived in a clearing where a number of solid houses, positioned around a gathering place in the middle, were huddled between hibiscus bushes. Katie tried smoothing her hair back into place as she looked at the crowd of people chatting and laughing. Evening was descending fast and lanterns already threw a gentle glow over everything.

Ben spotted her and came across after grabbing a half-coconut shell containing a white milky drink on the way. She drained the contents in one go. It tasted unusual but, by now, she knew it was a welcome drink and part of island traditions. Ben nodded approvingly and introduced her to his wife, Sarah, and a never-ending stream of other people. Ben's wife had black wavy hair that hung down to her rounded hips. She had a generous smile and dark, friendly eyes. The garlands of flowers round her neck and in her hair were additional necessities for any Polynesian woman, and they looked wonderful. She took Katie under her wing and asked her about her family and where she came from. Other women nearby joined them and told Katie about themselves and their everyday happenings. Katie felt integrated and at ease. She eyed them all. 'I do envy you your fantastic sarongs. They are so brilliant and exotic. You all look like something out of a movie.'

Sarah took Katie's hand. 'Then why don't you wear one?'

Katie already knew how generous islanders were. She tried to back-pedal, but it was too late. Some other women followed them indoors. In minutes, they'd wrapped her in a patterned sarong and tucked the ends firmly into place. Katie tugged on a matching green top and viewed herself in the mirror. The women nodded their approval.

Outside she followed them and self-consciously hobbled along until she adjusted and began to walk comfortably and barefoot like everyone else. People were gathered in groups and sharing a meal. There was succulent meat from a small roasted pig, various kinds of fish covered in herbs and wrapped in banana leaves, and an assortment of vegetables. Katie tried portions of whatever they offered her and it tasted good. Laura had warned her not to refuse anything. Katie also knew that normally the person's social standing governed which piece of meat they got. Katie didn't ask where she stood in the hierarchy. Someone put a circle of frangipani on her head and a garland of it around her neck. She felt quite native.

She already knew that the islanders loved dancing. After the meal, the drums and guitar began to play and people started to sing and dance. Their arms and hands moved in a single wave of graceful movement. Katie sat cross-legged and watched in fascination. Daylight had faded completely. Golden flickers from the lanterns settled now and then on the chocolate skin tones of the faces and bodies as they moved in rhythm.

Eventually, they beckoned her to join them and put her between Ben's wife and one of his daughters. Katie forgot her inhibitions and swung her hips. She always enjoyed dancing, but this was something completely different. Co-ordinating the movement of her arms and her hips was an impossible task, and she was sure she must look quite wacky. She lost the rhythm several times and had to start again. When the music ended, the people grinned and clapped loudly. Her cheeks felt hot and the strong scent of the frangipani flowers was intoxicatingly sweet.

She drank thirstily and looked around casually. Daniel was leaning against a palm on the edge of the clearing. His legs were crossed at the ankle, his face veiled in the shadows. He gave her a thumbs-up sign. Guitar music began to play softly again. When she saw him talking to other people and coming in her direction, Katie decided to make a discreet exit. She didn't want to listen to any quick-witted comments about her appearance or her dancing. She looked around for Ben and hurried to join him.

'Thanks for a lovely evening and the chance to meet your family. I enjoyed every minute.'

'You're not leaving, are you? The evening has only just begun.'

'I was on the beach too long this afternoon. I feel pretty tired.'

'You've had too much sun I expect,

but I hope you'll visit us again real soon.'

'I'd love to. I'll say goodbye to Sarah before I go. Where is she?'

Ben pointed and she went, taking care to steer clear of Daniel.

Katie hugged Sarah. 'Thank you. I enjoyed everything immensely. I'll give Ben the sarong back next week, washed and ironed.'

Sarah's teeth sparkled in the firelight. 'Keep it. It looks good on you. Visit us, any time. Don't forget your clothes.'

Accepting the carrier bag, Katie hurried down the path towards the beach. Away from the village, the sound faded and the cool leaves bordering the pathway brushed her skin. She heard firm footsteps following her and hurried onwards. The hotel lights beckoned in the far distance. The sea was calmer and the waves made a gentle swishing sound. She couldn't see why, but the soles of her feet began to suddenly sting badly. She limped to a nearby palm trunk and sat down.

12

'Walking through the undergrowth bare-foot in the dark is asking for trouble.' Daniel's voice cut through the silence.

She'd have hidden in the greenery if she knew he was following her. She shot a glance in his direction. He stood half-hidden in the shadows on the crest of the beach. If he expected that she was hoping for a relationship outside office hours, he'd be disappointed. She wasn't looking for another Paul or a meaningless affair. According to Laura, he already had a steady girlfriend.

He was waiting for a comment, so she gave him one. 'Is it? Why?'

'There are tiny barbs with prickly seedcases all over the beach hereabouts. Didn't you notice them? There are also centipedes that nip when cornered, and our very own brand of small scorpions. Luckily they're not dangerous.'

'I wore sandals to get here, but didn't put them back on for the return journey. I didn't know about the barbs, so they're the problem. Don't worry, I'll manage!'

His shirt gleamed white in the moonlight. 'I noticed you dancing back there. It was very attention-grabbing, but when I realized you were leaving, I saw you were barefoot and I wondered if you knew about the barbs. I decided to make sure. It's a fair distance from here to Rockley. If you can cope, I'll go back to the party.'

Katie got obediently to her feet and bit her lips. He'd go away if he saw she could manage. She did, for a few steps, but then she started hobbling on the edge of her feet again.

He came across and sounded triumphant. 'As I thought! You're a mulish woman! Why not admit that you're in trouble?' He chuckled. 'I can't help much here; it's too dark. We can return to Ben's, or go on. I think we'll opt for the hotel. The lighting is better once we get there.'

The hotel seemed far away and she was about to oppose the suggestion when he settled the matter. To her surprise and embarrassment, he lifted her up into his arms and shifted her around into a comfortable position. He began to walk down the empty beach and Katie's heart pounded like one of the village drums she'd left a few minutes ago. One arm supported her knees and the other curled around her bare ribs. His breath touched her face and his nearness was disconcerting. He looked down at her and grinned seductively.

'Put me down. This is ridiculous. It's not necessary. I can get back under my own steam. Go back to Ben's party.'

He ignored her. His grip tightened and he carried on. Raucous sounds of music and laughter drifted towards them from the hotel terrace. Katie knew how determined he was so she zipped her mouth and gave in. She wanted to escape from him, but how? She held on to his shoulder gingerly with one hand and gripped the carrier bag with the other. The perfume from the frangipani flowers drifted between them. It was strong and heady.

Katie wondered why she felt so hot and bothered as they moved along in silence. Daniel slipped now and then. Gradually, his pace slackened. His gaze dropped from her eyes to her shoulders and further down. He lowered her onto the sand and cast an approving glance at her tanned thighs in the moonlight. Katie tugged the material back into place.

'How much do you weigh?'

'A sack of potatoes, plus a few pounds.'

He chuckled. 'I'm either out of training or it's further than I thought it was.'

'This is ludicrous.' She looked up at him and tried to ignore the magnetism building between them. She listened to the waves hitting the sand and told herself he was, beyond any doubt, the wrong person. With the right person, it would have been a very romantic situation. She wondered if he was comparing her to other women. The thought was disquieting. At the moment, he was trying to be a knight in shining armour saving a damsel in distress. Thinking about armour and the tropical surroundings she was in, the laughter bubbled up from within her. The memory of his initial arrogance dissolved completely when he joined her laughter without asking what she was laughing about.

He collapsed onto the sand near her and she made a quick appraisal of his features. Nature had been very kind to him.

He spoke in a jesting quip. 'We'll carry on in a minute. I should've gone out to the firmer sand, bordering the sea. Relax, and enjoy the view. There's the Southern Cross.'

'Where?' He pointed, and Katie followed the direction of his finger to four bright points among a myriad of others. 'The heavens here are fantastic. It's odd to think that some of the stars don't exist anymore, even though we still see their light.'

'It's enough to see them; don't think about them exploding and disappearing forevermore. Just enjoy the moment for what it is.'

She looked sideways at him. 'That's your maxim, isn't it?'

'Perhaps! It's true that I don't worry much about the future or the past. You can't change the past, or the future. You can try to avoid trouble, but there's no guarantee that you'll never face any. The way you handle life right now is what really matters.'

'And how you cope with it?'

'Yep! It's stimulating that we don't know everything we should, and aren't always in control. No one can ever be sure how things will end. I enjoy cutting my way through the jungle. My way probably wouldn't be right for someone else, but I hope it's right for me.'

'And you never choose the wrong way?'

He chuckled. 'Of course I do; everyone does. You only know that it was wrong in hindsight, and then it's too late anyway. I just hope I don't make too many bloomers, or cause too much trouble for others on the way.'

'I've always tended to worry too much. I know it's stupid and useless most of the time, but you can't change your basic character, can you?'

'I'd rather be with someone who worries about what they're doing, than someone who doesn't think about the consequences, or care a damn. You're doing okay, Katie. Don't change just to fit; it never works. Just be yourself.'

She studied his face and swallowed hard before she pleaded, 'Surely I can manage the rest of the way alone now? It's not far.'

He shook his head and his smile flashed in the darkness. 'No. You'll end up shuffling, or crawling along on all fours. I can't allow visitors to believe we've got an intoxicated manageress.'

He got up and lifted her again, moving her around until she felt comfortable in his arms. He studied her face briefly, and grinned. He continued to walk on the soft sand, even though he'd admitted that the sand was firmer nearer the sea. The palms cast shadows across his features and veiled his expression. He reminded her of a pirate carrying his booty. He strode on and they neared the terrace. His physical nearness disturbed her more than she cared to admit. A lump blocked her throat. He certainly had charisma. She understood better now why he was a danger to any woman's peace of mind.

Katie concentrated on the beach and the ocean. The moon was an imposing globe of light throwing a silver trail across the sea's surface. Reaching the steps, Daniel acknowledged an astounded waiter with a brief nod, and moved between the tables. Some guests recognized them. They smiled and waved. Katie rippled her fingers at them and wondered what they thought.

Daniel's mouth twitched in amusement and then he chuckled. 'Look at their faces! They're speculating like mad.'

She didn't comment and tried to look

unconcerned as he continued on through the garden towards her bungalow.

'Which one? I've forgotten.'

'Twenty-five.'

He carried her up the steps. 'Where's the key?'

'In my skirt, in the plastic bag.'

He set her down. The circle of frangipani fell from her head. She ignored it and rummaged for her key. Her galloping pulse began to normalize. She looked at him towering over her, his back to the light, his face hidden. 'Thanks for your help. I'll be all right now.'

'You don't know what to look for, and you can't see the bottom of your feet.'

Defiantly, she replied, 'I'll manage.'

'Not unless you do regular yoga exercises.' He took the key, unlocked the door and pushed it open. His hand snaked around the doorframe and the lights came on.

He picked her up and her embarrassment resurfaced. Turning sideways, he carried her inside and deposited her on the bed. The mattress bounced her softly up and down. She felt at a decided disadvantage. Lying on the bed, with Daniel McCulloch looming over her, wasn't an everyday happening. He might feel at ease with a stranger in the bedroom. She didn't.

He squatted down to examine her feet. 'Let's see. Aha! As I thought. Got some tweezers?'

Katie gave in. 'Yes, in a pink-coloured cosmetic bag. It's on the shelf above the wash basin.'

Placing a chair at the foot of the bed, he sat down. 'Relax!' He was completely at ease with the situation. She wasn't, but protest was pointless. She lay on the pale blue bedspread and tried to ignore him. She finally took a stealthy look at him. He was concentrating on his task. In the end, she remarked, 'My feet must be disgustingly filthy.'

'Very!' He smiled lopsidedly, and her heart pounded. 'But I know why.' He continued to extract the tiny barbs, dropping them into his empty palm.

'I didn't want to dance but Laura told me it was rude to refuse. Among those graceful, swaying bodies, I must have looked weird.'

'You managed okay for the first time. It's an island tradition. The way you swung your hips was impressive. You looked quite sexy.'

She met the glint in his eye and saw the quirk of his mouth. 'If we had a night club on Naraotoa that offered table dancing you'd be the hit of the season. I think that's it.' He tipped the bits onto her bedside table. 'Got any disinfectant?'

'Yes, bathroom cabinet, on the top shelf. It's a small brown bottle.' She sat up, removed the frangipani garland and dropped it onto the floor. The edges of the white petals were already turning brown, but the fragrance filled the room.

Daniel returned and squatted to wipe the soles of her feet with the towel before he swabbed them with the disinfectant. Noticing her twitching feet, tongue in cheek, he remarked, 'You're very ticklish, aren't you?'

'Aren't we all? I'll kick if you carry on much longer.'

He smiled softly and stood up. 'In that case, give your feet a scrub before you go to bed. Wipe them over with the disinfectant again, to be safe.' He dried his hands on a corner of the towel and threw it on the bed.

Colour raced across her face. 'Thanks! How will you get back?'

'I'll get someone to drive me. Night! See you tomorrow.'

Her expression relaxed as the distance between them lengthened.

His size filled the room. He exited leisurely without looking back. 'You've got neat feet.'

13

When Katie woke, she felt buoyant. Thinking about last night, she wondered if she'd been too hasty. Rumours said Daniel knew exactly how to manipulate women but he'd been kind to her, shared her sense of the ridiculous, and behaved like a perfect gentleman.

Ben was sorting the mail.

'How are you this morning, Ben?'

'Don't ask! I have the daddy of all headaches.' He handed her some letters and added casually, 'You got home all right?'

'Yes, apart from picking up prickly barbs. Mr. McCulloch helped me.'

'So I heard. Daniel didn't return after he went looking for you. Someone just told me he carried you across the terrace in his arms.' He began to whistle softly.

Katie coloured. 'I wanted to come

back on my own, but he insisted on helping.'

Ben chortled. 'The gossips are busy because no one saw him leave. Daniel's already in the office.'

She wanted to quash the silliness but couldn't find the right words, so she moved on. The coffee machine was bubbling when she reached her office. After flipping through the envelopes, she tossed them onto the desk and filled her mug. Holding it between her hands, a slow smile materialized. She was flattered. Did people think she was attractive enough to attract Daniel?

He came in and sat down in the visitor's chair with a sheaf of papers in his hands. He slapped them onto the desk. Leaning back, he locked his hands behind his head and arched his back. 'How are you?'

Their eyes met and Katie hid her confusion. She'd gone from thinking about him to facing him in seconds. She sat down and folded her legs under her chair. 'Fine, thanks.'

'Good!'

She cleared her throat. 'Ben just told me that no one saw you leave, so they now assume I'm a femme fatale who's trying to ensnare my boss.'

His eyes twinkled briefly. 'Take my advice and ignore it. If you protest, they won't believe you. The more you bellyache, the more convinced they get. Their tittle-tattle will die faster if you pay no attention.'

'How did you get home?'

'I met a friend in the lobby; he gave me a lift.' He nodded towards the papers in front of him. 'Let's get down to business. I've a bone to pick. You're falling down on the job. Contrary to Lesperon's beliefs, we are not running the world's most exclusive restaurant. If you don't put a stop to his hanky-panky, it'll rip holes in our profits. He's taking advantage of you because you're gull-ible.'

She'd hoped for something better this morning, some increased friend-liness. Disappointment washed over her.

He'd said last night that he took each day as it came. Yesterday he was a friendly male; today he was a fault-finding boss. She forced her mind to focus on the restaurant's financial standing and hoped she sounded sensible. 'I noticed he was overspending and I told him so last week. I don't have time to check his budget daily. How can I control him?'

His brows were drawn in a straight line and his features were unsmiling. 'You've let it drift too far. You should've stopped him ages ago. A trained hotelier would have spotted it automatically.'

She coloured slightly. Daniel made it sound as if she was the problem, not Lesperon. He was nit-picking and probably enjoyed finding her blunders. She wondered if he appreciated that she'd made a real effort to come to terms with her job.

Her features were bland but her eyes mirrored her disappointment. She got up glanced out of the window, folded her arms across her chest, looked at him briefly, and then bent to pretend to study the papers.

'Check him unexpectedly; it doesn't need to be daily. Make him calculate his costs. Show him where he can save money. Keep at it. When he sees you're in control, he'll give up. If he doesn't kow-tow in the next week or two, I'll collar him but if you sort it out, it'll mean fewer problems for you in the future.'

'Okay. I'll try to curb him and keep you informed.' She avoided his eyes, gathered up the papers and shoved them into an empty folder. She pretended to look at her watch, and tidied a folder lying askew on the desk. 'Anything else? If not, I want to see Mrs. Hicks. I promised to help co-ordinate today's schedule from her office.' It was a lie, but she wanted to escape. 'The letters, and the brochure from the printer, are on your desk.'

He nodded impatiently. 'Yes, I know. I've gone through them already. I'll be in late tomorrow.'

Katie nodded and went towards the door. She left quickly, glad to get away.

14

Daniel shifted awkwardly in his chair. He picked up a pencil and played with it while gazing at Katie's untouched coffee. A film covered the surface. He should have told her it wasn't the first time Lesperon had gone wild.

He recalled the golden flecks in her green eyes and her disillusioned expression. He felt uncomfortable. He hadn't meant to sound insensitive. He wished he'd been more diplomatic. She ran the hotel proficiently and knew how to exert pressure and get things done without provoking the staff. In fact, things were working out better than he ever expected. He'd enjoyed the chance of getting to know her a little better last night. He'd glimpsed a relaxed Katie and liked their moments of fun.

He got up abruptly. He tried to focus his annoyance on the cause of all the fuss. He would have fired Lesperon long ago but for the fact that he was a first-class chef.

He hadn't realized how restrictive Sharon's presence would be. She had put him in a bad mood this morning when she phoned and warned him not to get too close to Katie. He now realized he'd passed his anger onto Katie. He'd enjoyed a free existence until now but Sharon expected him to be just as ambitious and dedicated as she was. It was the first time since he'd agreed to help that he realized how inhibiting this whole issue was personally. Clearly, Sharon had already established a network of informers, otherwise she wouldn't have already heard about last night. He exhaled audibly. Blast it! He thrust papers haphazardly into his briefcase and left hurriedly.

15

On her way to see the housekeeper, Katie felt glum. When Daniel offered his hand, it was a steel fist in a velvet glove. She only wished he wasn't so gritty and critical. Nobody was perfect. She could do without his friendship, but it'd be easier if he guided and encouraged, rather than attacked and criticized.

She listened with half an ear when Mrs. Hicks told her that a group of South American visitors were throwing heaps of money around, but living in a shoddy rented house on the outskirts of Varua. 'If you're a tourist with plenty of money, why stay in substandard lodgings?'

Absentmindedly, Katie said, 'It does seem strange, but perhaps they don't want people fussing around them all the time.' She got up and went to the window. Daniel's car was gone. 'I'd better get back to work. Thanks for the tea; it was just what I needed.'

★ ★ ★

After work, she changed and borrowed a bike. The exercise helped her forget work for a while as she pushed the pedals faster. It drove the frustration out of her system and brought colour to her cheeks. She barely noted the people she passed on her way. She cycled round the island, taking short cuts now and then or resting to view something new.

By the time she neared the hotel again, she was feeling a lot better. Without warning, a jeep shot out of a side road. They tried to avoid each other, but Katie flew over the handlebars and landed on the gravelled ground. The bicycle crashed on top of her. She felt foolish as she disentangled herself and scrambled to her feet. A good-looking fair-haired man in his early thirties with brown eyes and dressed in shapeless shorts and a polo shirt jumped out of the car.

'Bugger it! Are you okay? The road is busy mornings and evenings, but it's rare to see anyone here at this time of day. Everyone uses the other side anyway, because the surface is better over there. Sorry! I know it's not a good excuse, but it's the only one I've got.'

He seemed genuinely sorry and Katie couldn't be angry. Still feeling winded and slightly shocked, she said, 'It's okay. I'm all right.'

'Sure?'

Katie inspected her skinned elbow, scratched hands, and cut knees. Her cheekbone also felt numb, but she flexed her arms and limbs and shook her head. 'It's all superficial damage. I'm fine.'

He held out his hand. 'I'm Colin, Colin Walton. I live here.'

Katie smiled. 'Hallo. I'm Katie, Katie Warring.'

'You're the new manageress at the Rockley, aren't you?'

Her brows rose inquiringly.

He explained, 'Everyone knows Daniel

has a new manageress. I expect you already know how nosy people are on this island.' His eyes twinkled roguishly.

Katie liked his laid-back attitude. 'Yes. It's amazing. You know who I am and where I work, but I don't know you. That's not fair.'

He chuckled. 'Yes, it's annoying, I'm sure.' He paused. 'The least I can do is to drive you home.' He eyed the bike. The tire was flat and the wheel-rim completely twisted. His glance returned to her slim figure and her dust-covered sandals. 'Are you sure about the hospital?'

She nodded. 'Definitely!' She decided to accept his offer. 'A lift would be super if I'm not taking you out of your way.'

His muscular arms lifted the bicycle into the back of the open jeep and he helped her into the passenger seat. The journey didn't give them much time to talk.

He told her a little about himself on the way. 'I have a gift shop in Varua. I sell the usual things — shells, beads, postcards, scarves, and keepsakes.'

'Does it pay?' All the hotels had small kiosks with souvenirs and paperbacks. Katie was surprised he made any profit. He'd need unusual things to be competitive.

He grinned. 'I live on a financial knife-edge, but I'm optimistic. I'm in the process of buying my own plane, to bring stuff from the mainland.'

'That's an expensive outlay, isn't it?'

'Oh, I'll use it for other things too, and take on jobs whenever I can.' He had an infectious smile. 'It'll work out in the end.'

Katie thought his plans sounded uncertain but presumably he knew the island better than she did. 'Next time I'm in Varua, I'll come in and browse around.'

'Do. I'm on the main street, near the post office.'

By the time they reached the hotel, she'd decided that Colin was a very relaxed character. Evenly tanned, tall and long-limbed, his clothes proclaimed him to be what he was, a carefree man with a ready laugh. Katie liked him. Perhaps the episode with Daniel that morning had heightened her need for companionship.

He hoisted the bicycle out of the jeep. She pointed towards a nearby wall. 'Leave it there, please. I'll organize the rest.'

'Send me the bill.'

'That's all right, but thanks anyway.' She smiled.

'Don't thank me. I almost flattened you into a pancake. I'll be more careful in future.'

'Don't fret. Nothing serious happened. Thanks for the lift.'

'Despite the accident, I hope to see you again soon?'

She smiled. 'On an island of this size, I think that's very likely. Goodnight.' She turned to go. Reaching the glass doors, she looked back. He was still watching. She waved before she went inside.

Amos was on duty. His eyes widened

as she limped in. 'Lord! What happened to you?'

'An unexpected encounter with a jeep! Do me a favour, Amos, please. Take the bike back to the shed. I've left it outside.'

He nodded thoughtfully. 'Perhaps you should go to the emergency department at the hospital?'

'I'm okay. Just cuts and bruises, and my tetanus jab is up to date.'

'Certain?'

She nodded.

He decided not to argue. 'Phone if you need something.'

She limped away, took a shower and cleaned the cuts. Last night it was trouble with her feet; tonight other bodily parts hurt even more. She got into bed gratefully. She reflected on her meeting with Colin. She reached for a paperback and tried to ignore the throbbing. Tired from the exercise, she soon fell asleep with the book in her hand.

★ ★ ★

Next morning, she got out of bed and hobbled to the window to greet a perfect golden sunrise. Her kneecaps felt cemented into place. It took willpower to get ready for work. She zipped herself warily into a pale beige skirt that skimmed her knees before she realised she'd chosen the wrong length. Everyone would see the cuts and scratches, especially if the skirt slid up her thighs. She cursed Daniel's rules about trousers.

She checked the time and thought about changing into a longer length, but the prospect daunted her. A glance at her face in the mirror didn't improve her mood either. Her right cheekbone was a mixture of purple, red and blue blotches, and her bottom ached from the unaccustomed pedalling. The cuts had dried up during the night but they split open on her way to breakfast. She tried not to limp on the way to the office and hoped they had a first-aid kit in reception. If not, she'd have to go back to her room for some plasters.

A swollen wrist and aching elbow made even simple typing jobs challenging. She thanked providence that Daniel wouldn't be early. She could finish his work before he arrived. Checking her watch, she decided to dodge him if she could. A carpenter had an appointment to examine some damaged furniture that morning. It provided her with a perfect excuse; she'd go there. Daniel's work completed, Katie scribbled a note to tell him where she was and left it on top of the folders. She was waiting for the lift when he arrived. Instead of going to the office as she hoped, he came towards her. Blast it!

He glanced around the foyer briefly on the way, checking. When he reached her, his eyes took in the crusty marks and plasters on her legs and the facial damage. His brows formed into a straight black line. 'Whatever happened to you?'

Reluctantly, she said, 'I fell off a bike.'

He looked startled but his eyes twinkled. 'That's all? You look like you've battled with a prize fighter and lost.'

He seemed almost amused. He waited for her to give him the details and she told him exactly what happened.

'You're lucky you weren't seriously injured. Colin is a goddamn menace.'

'He isn't. We were both to blame. He brought me back afterwards.'

His angular features tilted slightly. 'Your cheek is a beautiful shade of purple. Does it hurt?'

Her hand automatically touched it, and she retorted, 'What do you think? Of course it hurts.' She wanted to escape. 'I've left your work on your desk.' She walked into the open lift, trying not to limp.

He followed and slapped his hand over the control panel. 'Come on. I'll take you up to the hospital to let them take a look at the damage.'

She said emphatically, 'I don't need hospital treatment.'

With laughter in his voice, he shook his head and muttered, 'The hotel pays for your health care, and I've decided you need attention. If you don't come of your own accord, I'll pick you up and carry you out to the car.'

She knew it was no use. She gave in.

At the hospital, Daniel asked for David. Thirty minutes later, she returned to the waiting room with David.

Daniel was busy with his iPad. He viewed her bandaged knees. 'That looks much better. Any other damage?'

David supplied the facts. 'Nothing serious. The cuts are already beginning to heal. We X-rayed her arm, but it's okay. A slight sprain, but that will disappear in a couple of days. We've given her some analgesic ointment and a couple of painkillers for the night if she needs them.'

Daniel nodded.

Katie placed her hands on her hips. 'Hey, I'm the patient. Don't give him information without my permission.'

David laughed. 'Try telling that to Daniel.' He ruffled her hair. 'Go home. And stay away from bikes for a while.'

She huffed and left them. Daniel's eyes were bright with merriment.

When they got back to the hotel, Daniel whizzed through the work she'd prepared for him. Before he left, he looked down at the white bandages. 'You can wear trousers until that lot has healed. I'd like those lovely legs in skirts again though as soon as possible!' Lifting his hand, he left with a smile and a flourish.

Later that day an extravagant basket of flowers arrived. The card just said 'Colin'. She placed it in a prominent position in her office.

Next morning, Daniel stopped on his way to his room. His eyes skimmed her bruised face and took in her crisp white blouse with the top two buttons undone and the dark blue trousers. He nodded his approval and then glanced at the opulent floral display and studied the card. 'He's a troublemaker.'

She retorted, 'That's your opinion.'

'I've known him longer. We're not on the same wavelength.'

'I can imagine.'

'Colin thinks life is one long carnival. Take my advice, and be careful.'

She busied herself with the papers in front of her. 'I always am.'

'Katie, take my warning about Colin seriously.'

'I'm always careful about the friends I choose.'

He stared at her for a moment and then disappeared into his office.

She continued to appreciate the wonderful colours, exotic shapes and perfume. She even took photos to send to her parents. She'd never received such a sumptuous bunch of flowers before.

* * *

Katie cornered Lesperon and told him that Daniel was on the warpath.

He gestured extravagantly. 'I try to economise, darling, but it's so difficult.'

'Perhaps you can use cheaper ingredients that are just as good?' Katie noticed his expression of disbelief and rushed on. 'If you don't reduce the costs, Mr. McCulloch will force you to change the menu, whether you like it or not. He's mad at you.'

Lesperon liked Katie. She'd been an au pair in France, and she spoke French quite well. She always listened to his problems. He sighed, but decided he'd help her out of a tight spot. Over the next couple of days, they settled on cheaper sources and rebuilt the menu. The dishes remained first class, and the catering costs fell to an approved level. Lesperon was smug, Daniel satisfied, and Katie relieved.

* * *

She and Daniel continued working efficiently. She was efficient and friendly, but determined to keep her distance after knowing how quickly his approach could change from positive to negative. He was her boss and he was Sharon's boyfriend; they were reasons enough to be wary.

Gradually the cuts healed and the bruises faded. She spent most of the day hidden away in the office, so her appearance didn't make much difference anyway. Daniel wouldn't notice if she'd dyed her hair three different colours on three consecutive days, as long as she did her work properly.

16

They were in the process of settling the details of a conference about the economic and environmental changes that might affect Naraotoa in the future. Daniel had set the wheels turning with the right people months ago. Tourism would remain the island's main source of income, but climate changes might bring other problems.

Daniel's rough organization plans lay scattered across his desk. Katie sat straight on the edge of the facing chair with a notebook in her lap. 'Who's financing it?' she asked.

He leaned back and his long fingers played with a pencil. 'The bank and the Chamber of Commerce are picking up the airfares and their expenses. The main speakers are in New Zealand for a similar conference. A friend in Greenpeace told me about them, and I thought it'd be a good idea to get them here. The one man is a German sociologist, the other is a French agriculturalist specialising in sub-tropical zones. I've also persuaded a well-known New Zealand conservationist to come. I provide the accommodation and the space for the conference.' He spread the papers out in front of him on the desk. 'I checked room reservations just now, and we're almost booked out that week. We had plenty of room when I fixed the date. I forgot to reserve rooms at the time.' He added grudgingly, 'My fault. Any suggestions?'

Even though Katie thought the colour of his eyes was remarkable and understood why women were so attracted, she could focus on her work because of their detached professional relationship. Some bosses covered their ineptitude with flattery, raillery and teasing. They might be easier to work for but their employees had to work harder to cover for them. On reflection, she preferred Daniel McCulloch. He had definite ideas,

114

took quick decisions and understood how to achieve his aims. Her lashes swept across her cheekbones. She fished out a folder and ran her finger down a list. 'Why don't we use the big family bungalow? It's still free and has three bedrooms, a sitting-room, internet connection and all the rest.'

He looked up and gave her a generous smile. Katie caught her breath and disquieting thoughts began to race through her mind.

'That's a great idea. Book it!' He checked his notepad. 'What about special menus? Necessary, or not?'

Katie added a note to brush up her French with Lesperon and see if the island library had any German language books. She now understood his reference to 'languages' at their first meeting. He wanted someone around to help with translating if necessary.

'Lesperon is back on the straight and narrow; he'll only over-spend if we let him create special menus. Perhaps we can ask him to make canapés for the mid-morning break? That'll pacify his ego without it costing too much. I notice they're staying a week but the conference is only for three days, isn't it?'

'There's only one scheduled flight every week, so we have to build their visit around that. They won't protest about an extra day to laze around.'

Katie pushed her hair off her forehead. 'Of course. I sometimes forget how isolated we are.'

Daniel pinched the bridge of his nose. 'Apart from the scheduled flight, there are supply ships, private airplanes, and helicopters. It's all we need at present.' He ruffled through the papers and gave her a hand-written list. 'These are the speakers and the themes. Type a rough agenda. Two hours for each topic. Split the rest of the time between discussions and question-time, a half-hour coffee break, and a lunch-break. We start at nine and it goes on until about two or three in the afternoon. If they need more time, we'll extend the schedule. If the discussion lasts too long, I'll have to curtail it as politely as I can.' Katie added some quick notes. 'I thought the party-room would suit; what do you think?'

Katie wasn't sure if he'd listen but he was in a very good mood so she tried. 'Wouldn't the children's playroom be better? There are only three youngsters booked for that week; I've checked. At this time of year, they'll be out on the beach all day. The playroom is larger, and it's more peaceful. It looks out onto the quieter part of the beach and any outside movements won't distract the listeners.'

He deliberated, and his white teeth chewed the end of the pencil. Katie noted that, apart from one slightly crooked tooth, they were undamaged. She ran her tongue over her lips and concentrated on his voice.

'True. Scantily dressed females would be diverting.' He grinned briefly. 'It's quieter on that side, because it's shadier. We'll have to move the toys out, but it's a good idea. Here's a list of people for an official invitation. They ought to get it before the weekend.'

She nodded. 'Right! I'll do it later today.'

'If everyone comes, the room will be too small, but I don't expect that'll happen. Most people will come out of curiosity or what interests them personally.' He drummed his fingers on the desk. 'I'll inform the newspaper and we'll put posters with the details in the bank, library and the post office to cover general interest.' She nodded and added another note to her list

★ ★ ★

Time sped by and Katie worked hard. She wasn't just busy preparing the conference; the hotel's day-to-day business had to function efficiently too.

On day one, the speaker from New Zealand was brief and to the point. The audience was soon involved in the discussion. Part of his talk centred on building typhoon shelters to accommodate the whole population. People looked grim as they considered the possibility.

Katie went to listen whenever time allowed. She found both speakers spoke excellent English. She wondered how much Daniel now regretted hiring her. His involvement impressed Katie. He attended every day. He was a demanding boss, but he was clever and clearly concerned about the island's future.

One expert, Jean-Paul Brouillet, offered practical suggestions to increase exports, and how to cope with globalisation. Katie began to share his coffee pause, and he soon began to search her out.

Daniel eyed them and a muscle flicked at his jaw before he turned away.

Katie always joined the visitors for the evening meal, and she enjoyed it. They led a strange life, travelling the world with no time to make lasting friendships. If islanders used a fraction of the ideas, it would be worth it.

Daniel planned to take his guests out to dinner on their final evening. When he gave his invitation, the Frenchman told him he already had a dinner date with Katie. Daniel's polite smile faded a little when he asked the other two.

Jean-Paul's attention flattered Katie. She enjoyed his company. They visited a small local restaurant overlooking one of the inlets. The food tasted good, the music was romantic, and her Gallic companion was charming. They talked about Paris and Brittany, where Katie once worked as an au pair for a couple of months. On their return to Rockley, they parted in high spirits in the lobby.

The group left next morning. Everyone shook hands with Daniel and Katie. Waiting last in line, Jean-Paul kissed her, French fashion, on both cheeks.

'Bye, Katie. Here's my address. Come to visit me next time you're in France.'

When the group left, Katie went indoors clutching his chit of paper.

★ ★ ★

Daniel strode to his car. With his foot heavy on the accelerator, he almost caught up with the taxi going towards the airport. He reduced speed, relaxed, and tried to concentrate on other things as he drove to the plantation.

17

Katie and Laura hadn't played golf since the week before the conference. Katie discovered that she enjoyed golf, but just for fun. She ignored Daniel's idea of getting professional instruction.

As the two women went around the course, it gave them a chance to gossip. Katie didn't gossip much, but Laura made up for it.

'I hear you've cemented Anglo-French relationships!'

Katie's mouth curved into a smile. 'What do you mean?'

'Oh, come off it, Katie. I heard about your romantic tête-à-tête in the Banana Boat and that you said goodbye with a kiss when he left Rockley.'

'Sorry to disillusion you, but Jean-Paul only took me out for a meal. The French always kiss friends like that. I'll probably never see him again.'

'Who knows? When you go home you might meet again, and fall in love.' She tilted her head to the side. 'If you do, I want an invitation to the wedding.'

Katie's eyes twinkled. 'If I marry Jean-Paul Brouillet, I promise to invite you. Okay? Perhaps there's already a Madame Brouillet, and a scattering of little Brouillets in France.'

Laura banished the idea aside with a toss of her head. 'Don't shatter my plans. I want an excuse to travel to Europe.'

'You don't need an excuse. You're welcome to visit me any time, promise.'

They shared a farewell drink on the terrace.

'How about coming to a barbecue we're having on Saturday? David has invited some people from the hospital. If there are only medics, they'll talk shop all night. Do come, Katie! Daniel's agreed to come. I haven't invited Sharon though, because I don't know if they're a serious couple or not.'

It was stupid to deliberately dodge

Daniel outside office hours. If she did it too often, Laura would scheme and conspire. 'Thanks! I'd like that.'

★ ★ ★

Before he left on Friday, Daniel offered Katie a lift. She knew he'd be passing the hotel anyway, so she accepted.

★ ★ ★

She waited in the lobby and went outside as soon as she saw his car. He was wearing a checked sports shirt and beige slacks. His hair was still wet from the shower and the sandalwood tang of his aftershave wafted across to her. Katie's simple, cool dress had a belt that emphasised her slender waist.

She got in and sank into the leather seat. 'Thanks for the lift.'

He glanced and merely nodded. The radio played softly and no one had to make small talk. They saw each other too often for that. When they reached the Stannards', the other guests were already there: a nurse, a junior doctor from New Zealand, and another young couple who were friends of the Stannards. Katie noted that the nurse eyed Daniel with interest. He gave her no special encouragement. Katie mused he wouldn't be fishing for anyone new at the moment anyway because he already had a girlfriend. He sat opposite Katie and seemed to enjoy himself. Whenever their eyes met she had the feeling he was analyzing her in some way.

They ate succulent steaks, mouth-watering side dishes, and island-fruit salad with ice cream to round things off.

Jeff, the assistant doctor, brushed his hair to the side with long artistic fingers. 'Someone recommended a bar called the Hideaway. I'm going next Saturday. Anyone else interested?'

Judy agreed swiftly. 'Count me in.'

David and Laura shook their heads. 'It's very loud and always packed with people.'

Daniel replied, 'Saturday? No, I'm doing something else I'm afraid.'

'What about you, Katie?'

Daniel wouldn't be there. 'Yes, why not?'

Jeff looked pleased. 'Good! Shall we meet outside, about eight?'

Later in the evening, Judy asked, 'Do you play tennis, Katie?'

'Yes.' She smiled. 'But not very well.'

'That's good, because I'm a beginner. Like a game one day?'

'Yes, I would.'

'I haven't got my working schedule with me, but if you give me your telephone number, I'll phone to fix a day.'

'Fine.' Katie rummaged in her bag for a piece of paper.

Laura's impetuous nature carried David's quieter character along. They talked about Ian's first experiences of university, about local happenings, and about a plane crash in Thailand. Everyone lingered. Finally, they thanked their hosts and left. Katie waved to the others walking to their homes in the town, as

126

they drove past. Daniel's car sped down the empty roadway.

The evening breezes tangled her hair as the car picked up speed. She enjoyed the feeling. Up above, the sky was cloudless and full of bright stars. Daniel pressed a button to automatically close the roof and they were blanketed in semi-darkness. Katie felt obliged to say something.

'It was a lovely evening. I like Laura and David very much.'

Daniel shook himself out of his reverie long enough to say, 'Yes, so do I.'

Katie presumed his thoughts were now centred on Sharon. Nightclubs and bars were always busy until the early hours of the morning. Perhaps he was meeting her later. She wondered why he didn't tell people Sharon was his girlfriend; then she'd be included in any of his invitations. The car soon reached the hotel.

18

'There's no need to drive up to the entrance. Drop me off and carry straight on.'

'Sure?'

Katie nodded; a slight, dark silhouette in the passenger seat. Daniel was surprised when she held out her hand. 'Thanks again for the lift,' she said.

The feel of her hand in his made Daniel grip it more firmly than he intended. The pantomime of shadow and the moon's glow made her silhouette look perfect, and somehow it begged him to touch her. Her eyes sparkled in the darkness, and her lips shone in a way that made the air catch in his lungs. He pulled her closer. She lay captive and powerless, her arms folded against his chest. He gazed into her face, noting the surprise. He followed his instincts and kissed her. The kiss sent the pit of Katie's stomach into a wild swirl. They studied each other across the shadows for a few seconds in silence, and then Daniel freed his grip. Katie slithered away from him across the leather seat and wrenched the door open quickly.

'Sorry, I guess I had no right to do that. Habit I'm afraid.' He knew it was a feeble excuse and a stupid thing to say, but he had to offer her something. He hoped to defuse the situation with flippancy. Normally, he needed to feel strongly attracted and welcome before he kissed anyone. If Sharon found out, she'd make him walk barefoot over hot coals.

Katie said quietly, 'I expect old habits die hard. No doubt the island is full of girls you've kissed and forgotten, but kissing is a waste of time unless you really like someone, isn't it?'

His answer came out of the darkness like a shot out of a pistol. 'A waste? A kiss is never a waste; it's the first step on the eternal search.'

'For what? It wouldn't surprise me to

find you're only looking for sex, not for a steady relationship. As long as someone is available, you don't seem to care who it is.'

'Sex keeps the world turning.' His voice was low and taunting. For some reason he wanted to goad her.

'You may as well spend your time in a brothel if that's all you want.'

He replied in a mocking tone, 'There isn't one on Naraotoa.'

She stepped back and slammed the door. 'Goodnight. I'll see you on Monday.' She hurried through the gates and up the driveway.

Daniel watched her from the darkness of the car. Every time she passed one of the flickering torches, it showed her clearly for a few seconds. He ran his hand over his face and gripped the steering wheel. He was confused and also furious with himself. A boss who sexually harassed an employee was despicable. Looking at his face in the car mirror, he wished he could turn back the clock, but it was too late now.

19

Sleep evaded Katie for a long time. She unsuccessfully tried to ignore the memory of Daniel's kiss. His offhand attitude and flippant remarks just made her feel shoddy. She hadn't flirted, and he'd dubbed the kiss as a mere habit. It'd be easier to accept if he'd said he liked her, but a habit just bunched her together with any other woman he knew. Katie imagined Daniel McCulloch as a lover. The idea wakened wicked devils in her solar plexus.

She swallowed the lump in her throat. She was confused and also worried about how to cope tomorrow. He'd created a stupid situation.

Just before lunch, she answered a knock on the door and found Daniel carrying a fat green bottle and two glasses. Feeling uncomfortable and baffled by his appearance, she didn't know what to say.

He looked ill at ease too. 'I assure you that I don't generally behave like I did last night. I didn't mean to be offensive. I'm sorry!'

She moistened her lips and uttered, 'The most sensible thing for us to do is to forget it ever happened. If we don't, we'll pussyfoot around each other and feel constantly embarrassed.' Her heart skipped a beat as she met his glance. 'It wasn't important. We seem to create devils in each other sometimes, don't we?'

'That's generous of you. I don't know why it happened.' Putting the glasses on the table, he poured the champagne. He handed her a glass; Katie took it and sat down.

He lifted his. 'Here's to us, and avoiding misunderstandings.'

Katie nodded silently and took a sip. He labelled it a 'misunderstanding'. It was more than that; it was a big mistake. He'd apologized, but left his motive unexplained. She decided not to query any further and to let sleeping dogs lie.

He leaned back and looked around. 'I used to live here. I quite enjoyed it, but I needed privacy and moved out.'

Katie took a sip and was relieved to converse normally with him. 'I understand that. Everyone thinks you're on duty twenty-four hours a day.'

He nodded and asked, 'But you like the work?'

She decided not to agonize about yesterday anymore. He'd watch his step in future. She relaxed a little. 'Yes, I love it. Who wouldn't? Although the job is fraught with strange moments sometimes, like today.'

He looked puzzled. 'What do you mean?'

Her eyes sparkled. 'I went for an early swim in the pool, and Mrs. Graham joined me. I could tell something was bothering her. I sense when visitors are ready to bare their souls; they have a certain expression on their faces. I expect you know what I mean.'

He nodded understandingly. 'And who is Mrs. Graham?'

'The Grahams are a nice retired couple in their seventies. They have a beach unit. I asked if everything was okay. She hesitated, and I made some more encouraging sounds. She admitted something was spoiling their vacation.'

'And? What was it?'

'I quote: 'The two next door are at it like rabbits all the time, and we can't get enough sleep because of the noise.' '

His eyes widened and he hollered out loud. Katie joined in the laughter and then continued, 'She didn't want to complain because she said she understood what it's like to be young and in love, but they needed their sleep.'

With his eyes still full of teasing laughter, Daniel asked, 'What did you do?'

'I said I'd move them to another unit. It's not so central, but it looks out onto the beach and it will be quieter. I've already told someone to help them move their belongings.'

Tongue in cheek, he asked, 'Are you going to lecture the culprits?'

She laughed. 'How? I can't tell them sex is forbidden, or put a limit on when, or how often.'

He spluttered and burst out laughing again. 'I see what you mean!'

'They're probably on honeymoon, or besotted with each other. They're leaving on Wednesday; I've checked.'

'I think the Grahams must be very tolerant if the other pair were at it like rabbits throughout the night, as Mrs. Graham put it. Others would've winged their way straight to the reception desk before breakfast next morning. Send them a basket of fruit and a bottle of wine on the house.'

She replied blandly, 'I've already done that.'

He nodded, and they eyed each other comfortably. The receptionist came up the steps.

'Afternoon, sir. I've been looking for you.'

'Hi Barry. Why?'

'There's a Miss Sharon Taylor waiting for you in the lobby.'

Daniel looked at his watch. 'Heavens! I forgot.' He smiled at Katie. 'I'm in trouble again. I'd better go.' He held out his hand. 'Forgiven?'

She gave him the ghost of a smile. 'Yes, of course. No harm done.'

He bounded down the steps and went off with Barry. Katie gazed at the champagne. She left it and went for a walk along a less frequented part of the beach. She thought about last night and about this afternoon. He was full of twists and turns.

The following week was quiet and Katie's apprehension faded. She tried to forget about the trip home from Laura's barbecue.

She met Judy, Jeff, and some others at the bar as arranged. The music blared and the place was too busy but Katie quite enjoyed it. She liked Jeff and enjoyed his attention. Katie liked Judy too. She reminded Katie about their game of tennis.

136

Judy asked, 'Is it still on?'

'Yes. What day? I can't make it before four thirty.'

'What about early Sunday morning? I'll book a court.'

'There are two courts at Rockley, but I'll come into town if you like.'

'That would be super! If we play for an hour, I won't need to rush back to change for work.'

'That's okay by me.'

★   ★   ★

On the way home after the game, Katie looked out of the bus window and felt happy. She liked Judy. They had a similar sense of humour and they agreed to play again very soon. She felt optimistic. Her job was working out, and she was enjoying Naraotoa and making friends at last.

20

Jeff phoned next morning. 'Hi!' he said. 'How about coming out for a meal one evening?'

'Yes, I'd like that.'

'Good. What about tomorrow? I've heard that the Pacific Rim is very good.'

★ ★ ★

When she arrived, Jeff was waiting. He spotted her and gave a slow whistle. 'You look great.'

Katie's dress of was of flimsy material in shades of lilac and she completed the outfit with delicate silver sandals. He tucked her arm through his and they went into the air-conditioned restaurant. Katie found nothing to criticize about the service or her surroundings. The conversation flowed without awkward pauses, and after the meal they went into the bar.

They'd been there a while when Katie saw Daniel arrive with a crowd. One girl clung to his arm and Katie presumed she was Sharon. A mass of tight curls were arranged tidily around a heart-shaped face, and her stylish clothes clung seductively to her neat curvy figure. Daniel noticed them.

Sharon studied Katie carefully before she gave Katie and Jeff a brief nod and turned away. Katie rippled her fingers at Daniel and hoped it was enough. She automatically compared his vitality and restless energy to Jeffs quieter, subdued personality.

Daniel came across. His black silk polo shirt rippled across his chest. He supported his weight on the back of the opposite chair.

'Hi! Never seen you here before.' His glance drifted over Jeff and lingered on Katie.

She lifted her chin. 'This is the first time we've been here.'

He shifted his attention back to Jeff.

'I heard you're a sailor. How about a cruise on Sunday morning?'

Katie played with the stem of her glass.

'I'd love to, but I'm on call this weekend.'

Daniel shrugged. 'Another time perhaps?'

'Daniel!' From the adamant tone, Katie guessed it was Sharon. Daniel continued to chat to Jeff about sailing. When he left, he nodded briefly to them both. 'See you tomorrow, Katie.'

Jeff was scheduled to go on duty at six a.m. She looked at her watch and then at his friendly face. 'If you're on early duty we ought to call it a day,' she said.

'It's not that late. I'll get you another drink.'

'No, I don't need one, honestly.'

'Okay, but I hope this won't be the last time?'

'I hope so too.' Katie meant it.

'Good.' He smiled. His eyes were warm and friendly

His borrowed car struggled its way back to the hotel and he helped her out. Warm tropical breezes caressed Katie's face and ruffled her hair. Jeff tilted her face and kissed her gently. His kiss felt warm, friendly, and undemanding. They looked at each other and smiled simultaneously.

'I'll phone,' he told her.

She nodded. 'I'll cross my fingers that you get home safely. That car is a nightmare.'

He laughed. 'You're right. You won't believe it, but I paid ten dollars to borrow it. I'll wring the owner's neck tomorrow.'

Katie laughed softly.

The clutch gave out a series of protesting screeches and smoke billowed generously before Jeff finally set off.

Katie went to her room. She thought about the evening. She enjoyed being with Jeff and hoped he'd ask her out again.

21

Katie was already busy with her work when Sharon called, wanting Daniel to phone her back. When he arrived, Katie handed him his folder and a bundle of messages.

He skimmed through them. 'Enjoy yourself last night?'

'Yes, thanks.'

'You weren't there when we left.'

She met his eyes briefly. 'No. We left early.'

He continued to read her messages. 'I'd better contact the bank straight away about this one.' He went into his office.

Sharon phoned again. She sounded impatient. 'Is Daniel there yet?'

'He just arrived.'

'Put me through, please.'

Katie glanced at the control panel. 'He's on the phone, but I'll remind him to call you as soon as he's free.'

'He's exasperating and needs to get his priorities right,' Sharon added. 'I hope I'm top of his list.'

Katie paused. 'I'll tell him as soon as he's free.'

'Thanks, Katie.'

★ ★ ★

A couple of days later, Katie felt pleased when Colin phoned. 'How are you?'

'Fine,' she answered. 'Thank you for the flowers. They were terrific.'

'My pleasure. I've been meaning to phone and ask you out for ages, but something keeps getting in the way. I'd like to make up for the accident.'

She laughed. 'There's no need for that. I told you so.'

'Then just see it as a perfect excuse for me to ask you out. I fancy you.'

Katie laughed softly. 'Well, in that case, how can I refuse?'

'You'll come? Good. Which would

you prefer, a meal or some native music?'

'The native music sounds fun.'

'Good choice. I'm flying to the mainland to pick up new stock for the shop on Wednesday. Back on Friday. What about the weekend?'

'Yes, fine.'

'I'm already looking forward to seeing you. I thought you'd come.'

Katie chuckled. 'You're very sure of yourself, aren't you?'

She heard the fun in his voice. 'Of course. That's why I outshine the competition. We'll go to Bob's Joint; it's a bar in Varua.'

Katie felt a twinge of disappointment but replied, 'Sounds interesting.'

'See you Saturday?'

'Yes.'

'Great! Bye, Katie.'

'Bye.' She looked forward to a happy-go-lucky evening. She leaned back. Why didn't he employ local women to make genuine souvenirs? They were clever with their hands and would be grateful for the work.

Katie was pleased. She'd had a date with Jeff, and now Colin had asked her out. She liked them both for different reasons.

Who needed nit-picking, disapproving Daniel McCulloch? He'd never mentioned her contract again; neither had Katie. Her salary was paid into her account regularly, so she was working to contract.

★ ★ ★

Next day, she played tennis with Judy after work and later on Jeff phoned to ask her out for a beer. They chatted easily. There weren't many customers in the peaceful bar. Katie told him about Paul and that she didn't intend to make the same mistake ever again.

When her taxi arrived, he kissed her goodbye but Katie felt no excitement.

22

Colin phoned on Friday afternoon.

'I'm back. What about our date? Does it still stand?'

'Yes, of course.'

'Good. I'll pick you up at half seven, okay?'

'I'll be waiting.'

* * *

Katie looked down towards the harbour. Daylight was fading and the fishing boats were bobbing on the water. Two silhouettes, wrapped in their own company, sat on the wall, looking out to sea and watching the sunset. She recognised Daniel and Sharon. Daniel glanced up the road and recognized them too. He got up and strolled up the hill with his partner at his side.

Katie wished he'd stay where he was.

Colin noticed him and waited expectantly. The two men had grown up
together but friendship was foreign to
them. The knowledge bounced uneasily
across her mind. Her lips formed into a
stiff smile and she hoped she looked
friendly. The gloom had robbed Daniel's
eyes of their bright blue colour and his
voice held smidgens of disapproval.

'What are you doing here?'

Colin scrutinized Sharon with interest. 'It's none of your business, but it's
obvious, isn't it?' He nodded towards
Bob's Joint. 'We're about to go in. Want
to join us?'

Katie avoided Daniel and looked at
Sharon. She could understand why Daniel
was attracted. She was a blond beauty
with a strong personality.

Momentarily distracted by a group of
youngsters lounging on the street corner,
Daniel shouted in irritation, 'Bobby, does
your mum know you're in town? Do
something brighter than hanging round
corners like a hobo.'

Bobby tried to look cool and appear

unconcerned. 'Like what?'

Daniel snapped, 'The youth centre is open till ten thirty. There's a free showing of *Mission Impossible*.'

They grumbled, but Daniel might tell their parents. They slouched off with their sneakers undone, pants at half-mast, and their baseball caps askew.

Satisfied, Daniel concentrated on Katie and Colin again and tipped his head in the direction of the club. 'That place is seedy.'

Was it the sound of his voice, or the strong breeze blowing from the ocean that produced the goose pimples on Katie's arms?

Colin countered, 'Is it? Who cares? I come here often. We intend to enjoy ourselves, don't we, Katie?' He draped his arm casually round her shoulders.

She didn't approve of Daniel interfering in other people's lives. She nodded at Colin and tried to sound involved. 'Yes.'

Daniel sneered slightly. 'There's no accounting for taste. Haven't you heard that the police raided the place the other day?'

'Did they?' Colin chuckled. 'No, but they've tried that before. I'm surprised they find the time. Normally they're too busy writing speeding tickets.' He viewed Daniel defiantly. 'There are plenty of other likely spots to check. Your warehouse, for instance.'

Daniel stiffened and his eyes glistened. His hand formed into a fist but Sharon quickly tucked her arm through his.

Satisfied with the effect he'd had, Colin continued, 'Don't worry, I won't lead Katie astray. We just intend to enjoy ourselves.'

'There are better locations. Why come here?'

The two men were like chalk and cheese. They didn't like each other and it showed. Katie met Daniel's eyes defiantly. 'I'm old enough to take care of myself, Daniel.'

He retained some shreds of cordiality, but his expression hardened. 'You may be, but Colin is not.'

Colin threw back his head and

laughed. 'You think you rule the roost but you'd be surprised who's really in control around here.'

'Think so? I don't rule anything. I just like living in a safe and comfortable environment.'

Sharon tugged at his sleeve. 'Daniel, let's go.' She gave a throaty laugh and captured his attention for a few seconds. He pressed his lips together and nodded silently.

Katie was taken aback. Daniel preferred to command and set the pace. He must be in love with Sharon to let her decide for him.

Colin's brown eyes twinkled. He clearly enjoyed provoking Daniel. Katie wanted to defuse the antagonism in the air. 'Are you going somewhere special?'

Sharon answered, 'We haven't decided yet.' She pushed some blond hair back into place. 'There's always Daniel's place if all else fails.'

The image of Daniel and Sharon making love in his bungalow shot through Katie's brain and gave her the collywobbles.

A muscle flickered at Daniel's jaw and he glanced briefly at Katie. 'Enjoy yourselves.' He disentangled his arm and turned away abruptly.

Sharon smiled at them. 'Bye!' She hurried after Daniel and tucked her arm possessively through his again. Their voices grew fainter as they wandered back towards the harbour.

Colin put an arm round Katie's waist and propelled her in the direction of the bar's entrance. On the way, Katie looked up at the sky and steadied her thoughts. It was hazy and decorated with silver stars. She walked bare-legged and bare-armed, and cool breezes plastered her thin multi-coloured dress to her body. She shivered; the prospect of spending a pleasant evening had vanished.

Colin remarked gaily, 'Daniel thinks he's unrivalled.' His voice sounded cheerful. 'I love baiting him.'

'You two act like kids. If you don't get on, why don't you just ignore each other?'

He hugged her and they went inside.

Dimly lit corners and flashing psyche-delic lights made it impossible to tell if the room was shabby or chic. Music filled the air, and there were too many people packed into the meagre space. Cigarettes and something much sweeter swirled through the air. Katie felt uncomfortable.

Colin knew everyone and everyone knew Colin. Raucous conversation and artificial laughter went on all evening. Katie soon looked forward to going home, although Colin seemed to be in his element. He didn't leave until most of his other acquaintances had already gone.

23

Colin pooh-poohed Katie's suggestion of going home by taxi. It was three a.m. He tumbled into the driver's seat and started the engine. Katie fixed her seat belt. His driving skills seemed unimpaired, but he'd been drinking. Colin sang along with a tune from the radio and turned to smile at her.

She said, 'That was a funny place. There was a flashily dressed chap in one of the corners. Perhaps the rumours about illicit dealings are true after all.'

Colin shrugged. 'Perhaps, but harmless stuff like hashish or speed, I expect.'

'Hashish isn't harmless. It's shady. Illegal pills are life-threatening.'

'Katie, some people are addicted to chocolate, or champagne.'

'That's not the same, and you know it. Soft drugs are not risk-free.'

'That's what people tell you who've

never tried them.'

'No one is stupid enough to stick their hands voluntarily into the fire. Anyone with any sense knows illegal drugs are harmful.'

He reached out one arm to hug her. 'Oh, Katie! Why worry? If people want to take these things, let them.'

She stared ahead. She disliked the idea Colin might be involved with drugs. Some of his friends looked like they lived in the twilight zone, but it was his life. He should know what he was doing.

Rounding a curve in the road, an off-road vehicle drove alongside. Colin steered towards the inside of the road. They were travelling along a narrow section. The sides were steep and of volcanic rock. The other car drove parallel with them for a few seconds. It was bigger and threatening and there was a broad-shouldered silhouette behind the wheel.

The two vehicles drew closer and Katie wondered if the man was drunk or just a bad driver. Colin had no room to manoeuvre. In a desperate effort to avoid sharper pieces of rock sticking out of the embankment, he spun and straightened the wheel and changed gears frantically. Creepers and greenery slapped greedily at their windscreen as they went past.

The off-roader roared and shrieked and closed in on them again. It scraped the side of the jeep and managed to push it sideways. Somehow, Colin kept in control. Katie gripped her safety belt as the two vehicles touched again. Panic was growing by the minute.

Just when she'd almost given up hope, they exited from the tunnel-like sector and Colin steered into a drainage ditch alongside the road. The other vehicle sped off into the night. A hand above the driver's cabin waved in the moonlight. It intermittently sounded its horn and disappeared round the next corner.

Silence reigned for a moment. Katie was shocked and asked breathlessly, 'Who in heaven's name was that?'

Staring into the darkness, Colin replied, 'No, idea. Probably some drunken idiot. Whoever he was, he's disappeared. Are you all right?'

Her heartbeat steadied. 'I'm okay. You should report him.'

He said sharply, 'Why? Nothing happened. Maybe my jeep has a few more dents, but it wasn't in good shape before.'

'He should be reported. He could have killed us!'

'I'd need to describe the vehicle in detail. It happened too quickly for noting numbers or anything else. Anyway, I've been drinking. If I walked into the police station, they'd do a breathalyser and I'll be up to my eyeballs in trouble.'

'There can't be that many off-road vehicles on Naraotoa.'

'More than you imagine. Oh, let's forget it.' He leaned forward to start the engine. It coughed once or twice and then sprang to life.

Katie's lips clamped together and she stared ahead. The evening hadn't been much fun. The bar was bad enough, but the journey home was even worse.

Outside the hotel and with solid ground under her feet again, she began to feel better. She managed to say thanks, although the evening had been a disaster.

'I'm sorry about what happened. Give me a chance to make up for it. We'll see each other again, very soon I hope?' He sounded genuinely repentant.

'If you can guarantee something quieter and less life-threatening.'

Colin leaned towards her and kissed her cheek. 'We'll go for a quiet meal next time. Okay?'

She waited until he drew away from the kerb and then she ambled past her bungalow to the deserted beach. She listened to the waves and watched the moonlight coat everything in a silver sheen. Nothing seemed to bother Colin. He made her laugh and she liked being with him, but there were aspects about his character that worried her.

She hoped he did have other friends she'd like more.

Katie wished she could talk to her sister. She looked up at the myriad stars in the sky and reflected that life had lots of surprises in store.

24

Daniel stared into the mirror with fierce concentration and guided the shaver impatiently along his jaw. His life these days was much too complicated; he'd lost control. He'd always enjoyed the company of women and, apart from Maureen who dumped him for an Australian farmer with a farm bigger than Naraotoa, previous relationships always ended without remorse when the parting came. He'd soon realized even Maureen hadn't been the love of a lifetime, but she'd changed his attitude. He'd been wary ever since, and although he knew that some girls hoped he'd fall for them, he'd never wanted to turn an affair into a long-lasting relationship.

He knew everyone was watching him and Sharon. That was how it was meant to be. It was their strategy. The authorities weren't doing this for the first time.

He knew people were speculating about the two of them. Sharon was interested in everyone and her intelligence and curiosity impressed a lot of people, but that was part of the job.

He showered and dressed. His thoughts drifted back over the weekend. Sharon seemed satisfied and happy with their findings so far. He shrugged unconsciously and went to the kitchen. Eating a slice of toast saturated with butter, he looked at the riot of purple bougainvillea rampaging wildly down the slope. He thought about Colin and Katie and nearly burnt his fingers on the steam from the kettle.

Daniel arrived at the office with a tight-lipped expression on his face. He uttered a clipped greeting and went straight into his room. Katie followed with his coffee mug and the signature folder. He hardly read the texts as he turned the pages and signed everything impatiently. He handed her the completed folder back. 'Just keep your eye on the cost, and do as you think best.'

Katie noticed his mood but didn't comment.

On his way out, he stopped by her desk and said, 'Be careful about spending too much time with Colin. I know him of old. He's impulsive and irrational. He's also a flirt and a playboy.'

She looked up and drew a sharp breath. 'It's none of your business, Daniel. I don't interfere with your private life, and I'd like you to stay out of mine. I can take care of myself. I choose my own friends. If Colin is a flirt, you're not in a position to criticise him. Rumour has it you're very renowned for your various amorous affairs.'

The skin on his cheeks tightened and a muscle shifted in his jaw. His eyes regarded her silently. He went out without replying and closed the door with an audible thud.

25

The hurricane season began and heavy storms swept the island. They increased in number and velocity day after day.

Laura's son came home on a visit. Ian looked like a taller, younger and thinner version of David. Katie imagined how he probably impressed the girls at his university. Ian had never-ending energy and plenty of charm. One afternoon, Judy and Katie joined forces to play tennis against him and he beat them ignominiously. Laura was down in the dumps after he left, but she bubbled back faster this time.

The work in the office continued in a hassle-free way. Katie and Daniel worked well together and he didn't control her as carefully anymore. She felt much better in his company because she was more confident. He had the will of an ox but when he quipped about something, his blue eyes sparkled, and she felt very light-hearted. She remembered their hostile beginning and admitted they'd come a long way since then. Nowadays, Katie knew when they had different opinions he either accepted her argument without comment, or patiently explained why he'd decided differently.

* * *

Jeff called one day to suggest another rendezvous, but phoned again later to postpone it. He had to accompany a patient to New Zealand for an emergency operation.

She arranged to play golf with Laura instead. Heavy rain showers interrupted them a couple of times. They broke off and shared tea in Katie's room.

Laura left, and Katie witnessed another heavy downpour of rain as it hit the concrete in front of the bungalow like a never-ending cascade of silver coins. Dark clouds tumbled across the sky, noisy thunder rolled in antagonistic waves, forks of brilliant lightning split the darkness, and the palm leaves circled in acrobatic gyrations. The storm vanished as fast as it came. Islanders ignored the weather and went about their business as usual.

An hour later, Katie was surprised when Laura phoned. 'Hi! Did you get home before the storm? Do they get any worse?'

Laura wasted no time. 'Katie, David just phoned. Daniel went cruising before the storm broke. He told someone he wanted to test something. Heaven knows why. He's a good sailor and knows how unpredictable the weather can be. They've lost contact. Some of the men plan to go looking. Katie, are you listening?'

Katie felt numb. Laura's voice sounded remote. She gripped the receiver fiercely. 'Yes. Where do they intend to go?'

'They don't know; they're taking pot luck. The wind could have driven him anywhere.'

She might never see Daniel again.

She pulled herself together and took a deep breath. 'That sounds bad.'

'Today's a very bad day. David was depressed even before he heard about Daniel. They admitted a youngster with an overdose of heroin this afternoon and we know the boy's parents quite well. It's appalling; everyone warns kids about taking drugs, but they still do it. David intends to call at the yacht club on his way home, to hear if there's any fresh news.'

Katie swallowed a lump as big as a rock. 'Let me know if you hear anything.'

'Yes, of course I will. Bye.'

With the receiver still in her hand, Katie tried to clear her thoughts. Perhaps he was on an outlying island. She was certain he wouldn't want people to make a fuss. She stared into the emptiness for a while before she got up. She had to tell Ben.

He already knew. Information spread across Naraotoa faster than a bushfire. All of Rockley's employees and a lot of other people on the island knew Daniel better than she did.

'Carry on as usual!' Katie said. 'No long faces and no gossiping. Daniel would hate that.'

Ben looked glum but nodded in agreement.

She found it difficult to use Daniel's name. She went to check the restaurant and the bar. The waiters smiled less, and the barkeeper wasn't so generous with his jokes, but the guests hardly noticed the difference. Katie went to the office. Work kept her hands busy even though her mind went round in circles. Ben stuck his head round the door to say cheerio. The skeleton night-staff began their shift. There was still no fresh news. Everything was up to date, so she went to her room.

Katie sat on the veranda, with her arms wrapped round her knees like a leprechaun. She stared into the darkness. Despite the humid temperatures, she felt cold and numb. Torrential rain showers hammered the roof and broke the silence now and then.

With every passing hour, her fears increased. She put on a thick sweatshirt and went for a walk along the empty beach. The wind whipped her clothes and slapped her hair in untidy bundles in front of her face. She barely noticed how the waves flirted with the thick soles of her canvas shoes. Katie walked until she was level with the church. She wondered if the door was open. When she turned the knob, the door gave way. The atmosphere helped and she sat until daylight flooded the interior. Outside again, she noticed a familiar figure on his way.

'Morning! Any fresh news?'

She shook her head. 'Not as far as I know. I'm on my way back. You're early!'

Ben nodded. 'I couldn't sleep.'

They walked side by side. 'You've known Daniel all his life, haven't you?'

'Yes. I went to school with his dad.' He glanced out to sea. 'We all thought that he'd sell the plantation when Jamie died. He didn't, and kept the people in employment. When Daniel went to university, his Dad and I knew he'd come back. The island is in his blood. He lent me the money for my son's training in New Zealand. People respect Daniel because he cares a lot about the community.'

They reached the steps leading up to the terrace and she glanced at her watch. There were sounds of activity from the kitchen and a waiter was setting the tables for breakfast. Ben left her and went towards reception. She needed to shower and change, but she sat down on the steps and leaned forward. Breezes from the sea cooled her skin, but went unheeded. She looked along the empty beach. The colours of the early morning sky were wonderful. A gathering of sea birds circled and took their morning exercise against a backdrop of golden grey. Everything was still and peaceful. Why couldn't today be like any other? A lump formed in her throat.

'Morning!'

She jumped and thought she was fantasizing. She wasn't. He looked extremely tired. His face was pale and haggard and he had a shadow of a beard. She sprang to her feet and flung her arms around his neck and burst into tears.

Surprised by her reaction, he rubbed away the tears from her cheeks with his thumbs. 'Hey! I may try getting lost more often if I get more of this treatment when I get back.'

Daniel's physical nearness comforted her. She felt the hard muscles and the warmth of his body. She saw the shadows under his eyes and the weariness in his face. She let go, and stepped back. 'What happened?'

The concern in her face startled, and also reassured him. She wasn't the ice maiden he thought she was. 'I misjudged the speed of the squall and when it hit, my position was all wrong to sail back. I let the yacht run. The main mast snapped in two. From then on, I lost radio contact. It took me

169

hours to sail home.'

She stared at him breathlessly.

'When I got back, there were lengthy explanations, and then I decided I ought to hinder you organising a remembrance service.' The corners of his mouth turned up.

Her voice was sharp. 'Daniel, it's not funny.'

He was quiet. 'I know. I've been out in storms before, but it was an appalling one this time.' He cleared his throat. 'Katie, I'm starving, I need food.'

Katie nodded and searched mechanically for a handkerchief. Daniel offered his. It was grubby but she took it anyway.

'I'll shower and be back in a couple of minutes.'

Katie watched him go and heard the staff shouting greetings as he passed. Her relief was physical. Her knees felt like rubber.

He returned, wearing fresh jeans and a clean polo shirt. She smelt the familiar fragrance of sandalwood. He still looked tired, but also more relaxed.

'Ben said he met you near the church this morning?'

Katie coloured. 'Yes. I thought an extra prayer might come in useful.'

'I'm not sure that I deserve it, but it may have tipped the balance up there. Perhaps you were my guardian angel? Share my breakfast; it'll taste better in company.' His blue eyes sparkled in his tired face.

She understood nothing about sailing but she listened carefully as he told her about the storm. Eventually, he leaned back in satisfaction. 'I'd better phone Sharon before someone else does.'

Katie nodded. The first guests were already arriving for breakfast when he left. She phoned Laura, but Laura knew already. Her work was also up to date, so Katie finished early. Tiredness swept over her and she fell into a deep, dreamless sleep.

She tried not to dwell on the happenings. Although Daniel generally never came on Saturdays, next day

Katie saw him chatting to some guests on the terrace. Katie wondered if he forgot an experience like that easily. She almost resented the fact that Sharon was the one to reassure and calm him.

★   ★   ★

On his return from New Zealand, Jeff phoned. They arranged to meet that evening. After talking generally for a while, he played with his glass and said, 'We're not matched for more than friendship, are we?'

They got on well and Katie realized she needn't fret about Jeff. He expected nothing. She met his eyes. 'No. I like you, but there's a big difference between friendship and love.'

'Yes. Perhaps it's just as well we're only ships passing in the night, isn't it?'

'Time and place doesn't matter if someone is right for you, but friendship is important too. Sometimes it lasts longer than a love affair.'

He laughed. 'You're right there. I'm

glad we're friends. You're one of the nicest girls I've ever met but if the chemistry doesn't work, one shouldn't pretend it does, should one?'

Katie shook her head. 'That would be a disaster.'

He lifted his glass. 'Here's to friendship.'

26

During their game of golf the following week, Laura took a swing at the ball and asked, 'Are you and Jeff serious?'

Katie realized that the grapevine was working overtime again. 'No. We're good friends. There's nothing special going on between us.'

'It's none of my business, but I don't think you two are suited. Jeff has a lot of excellent qualities, but you'll be happier with someone who provokes you from time to time.'

Katie smiled. 'Think so?'

'It's easy to end up with the wrong person. Just think about your ex-boyfriend.'

'Most girls would fall for Jeff at the drop of a hat. He's reliable, trustworthy, and he's a doctor to boot. He's nice too.'

'But he's not for you. You'll meet someone who makes you feel very special one day. He's out there waiting for you. Never consider second-best, ever.'

Katie grinned. 'I won't. Promise!'

*   *   *

Several guests had told Katie about a fantastic beach on the other side of the island. Katie and Judy decided to visit it. The bus service was erratic on Sundays, so they borrowed bikes and met at the turn-off to the beach. The sun blazed out of a cloudless sky. Murana Beach was indeed a beautiful place, and it was still comparatively empty.

Four small outlying, uninhabited islands on the horizon rested in a turquoise ocean, and dark coral reefs edged the lagoon. They spread their towels under the shade of some palms not far from the water's edge. Shedding their shorts and T-shirts, they ran into the water.

Afterwards, Judy decided she was going to snorkel. 'Why don't you come?

I've only tried a couple of times, but I love it. It's super.'

'Another time? I want to stretch out and relax.'

Judy grinned. 'Okay! I'll borrow the equipment and find the best spot for beginners.'

She went, and Katie lazed in contented silence. Judy came back and trickled water on Katie's midriff. Katie sat up and stuck her tongue out at her friend. 'You're a monster. And? Enjoy yourself?'

'The water is wonderful, but I hoped for more fish and more colour. The Sailing Club is over there.' She pointed. 'There are dozens of yachts along the jetty. You can hire small dinghies.'

'Can you sail?'

'No, can you?'

Katie shook her head.

'Pity! Doesn't Daniel own a yacht?'

'Yes. I'm not sure if it's here.'

'Considering that you work for a young, attractive boss, you don't know much about him, do you?'

She shrugged. 'I don't pry into his private life. Why should I?'

'Most women would. According to what I hear, he's quite a catch.'

Katie wanted to agree, but said, 'If you worked for him, you'd see things differently. Are you personally interested in the people you work with in the hospital?'

Judy chuckled. 'The interesting and attractive ones are married. The others aren't my cup of tea.'

'That's life, isn't it? You need a lot of luck to find Mr. Right.'

Judy flopped down and towelled her hair. 'And what's your idea of Mr. Right?'

'Same as yours I suppose.'

Judy grinned and then paused. 'You're dating Jeff, aren't you?'

She shook her head. 'No. We're not dating. Why do people assume such things? We're just friends. Hey, that's an idea. Jeff would suit you to perfection.'

Judy covered her head with a towel and rubbed vigorously.

'What about something to eat?'

Judy emerged again. 'Good idea! I'm famished. There's a nice little restaurant over there. The menu looks good, lots of dishes with local fish, and the prices are reasonable.'

They picked up their belongings and went across the soft sands. The cafe's wooden patio overlooked the beach and the sea breezes ruffled the tablecloths. They ordered a seafood dish and it tasted first class.

Someone else had bagged their spot when they wandered back, so they were forced to look elsewhere. Judy nudged her.

'Look! There's your Daniel.'

Katie looked up. He looked like a billboard advertisement in white shorts and a blue and white striped T-shirt.

'He's not my Daniel!'

He didn't notice them but when Judy greeted him, he stopped and came across.

'Hi, what are you two doing here?' His eyes narrowed to avoid the sunshine sneaking past the peak of his cap.

'People told us about this beach,' Judy said. 'We decided to try it.'

'It's not bad, but there are better ones on the other side of the yacht club.' He looked at the bundles in their arms. 'Are you going home?'

Judy wanted to gain his attention. 'No, we're looking for a shady spot out of the sun.'

It worked; he turned to her and smiled. Judy's eyelashes fluttered and Katie felt resentful. Why, for heaven sake? If Judy wanted to flirt with him, it was none of her business.

Daniel tipped his head. 'Go round that bend. There are some quiet beaches just out of sight.' He paused. 'Hey, I've an alternative. How about a cruise instead? I'm leaving after I pick up some rope from the shed.'

Katie was taken aback. 'You're sailing again? After what happened last week?'

His expression stiffened. 'If you fall off a horse, you climb back on. That's what I'm doing. When you sail, you reckon with good weather and bad, and technical hitches.'

Too annoyed not to retaliate, she said, 'But it's wiser to avoid unnecessary risks. Why do you have to go sailing today, after what happened? Storms still happen daily.'

Their eyes clashed.

'That's a stupid remark, Katie. Sailing isn't just calm seas and blue skies. I hope you're not suggesting I put my boat into mothballs during the rainy season. Anyway, it's none of your business. I calculate the risks and don't take deliberate gambles.' Ironically, he added, 'Much as I appreciate your concern, of course.'

Katie flushed and looked down.

Judy viewed them in bewilderment and said quickly, 'I'd love to come. A trip on the ocean would be wonderful.'

He gave Judy his undivided attention and she was a very appreciative audience. 'Tell you what. We'll sail to Matapa Reef. It's unspoiled by tourism.' His eyes scanned Katie briefly.

'What about you? Coming?' Even to his own ears, his voice held no welcome. He got the answer he expected.

'No thanks. I've been in the sun too long already.'

'There's an awning on deck.' He shrugged his broad shoulders and made no further effort. 'I'll get that rope and be back in a couple of minutes.'

Judy nodded excitedly. Without a glance at Katie, he strolled off.

'Are you mad?' Judy muttered. 'Why did you turn him down?'

She looked out to sea. 'Business and pleasure don't mix. Enjoy yourself, but I'll be gone when you return.' Katie smiled and tried to sound cheerful. 'As soon as it cools down a bit, I'll head for home.'

'I still think you're being silly. Why not say you've changed your mind?'

Katie shook her head. 'Because I haven't.'

Judy shrugged. 'I'll go for snorkelling equipment again. Will you wait here in case he comes looking for me?'

Katie nodded. She guarded their beach things and processed her anger. She blamed him, but knew it was her own fault. She'd turned down the chance to spend a terrific afternoon on the Pacific Ocean. Daniel and Judy came back together.

'Pity you're not coming.' He rubbed salt into the wound. 'David and Laura are on board, along with someone who helped me with the repairs to the mast. The forecast is good. I just checked.'

Katie turned away, and her voice drifted over her shoulders. 'Fine! I'll be off. Say hello to David and Laura. Enjoy yourselves.' She shouldered her bag and ambled off.

His look of irritation faded as she walked away.

* ★ ★

Katie spread her towel and threw herself down in a flurry of anger. She was mad at him, but mostly mad at herself. She'd slated him in front of

Judy; no wonder that he hit back.

She and Daniel seldom quibbled much in the office these days, so why did she still act crazily sometimes? If she'd swallowed her pride, she'd be with them now, skimming across turquoise waters. How did the saying go? Pride comes before a fall.

After pretending to enjoy herself, and frustrating the clumsy attempts of a tourist to flirt with her, she decided to leave.

★ ★ ★

Next morning Daniel stopped by her desk. 'Morning!' he said. 'Enjoy yourself yesterday?'

He was waiting for her to ask the appropriate questions, so she did. 'Yes, thanks. And — did you?'

'We had a great time! The weather was perfect. Judy snorkelled, David and Laura enjoyed a relaxing afternoon with some chilled wine, and I enjoyed playing guide and host.'

She busied herself with some papers.

He continued. 'I think we all enjoyed it.'

Katie managed to utter through clenched teeth, 'Good!'

Daniel picked up his post and whistled under his breath on his way to his room.

27

Late the following Sunday afternoon, Katie ambled along the beach in shorts and a top. She loved Sundays because she could go for a long walk parallel with the ocean. Lots of children played on the beaches as she passed the villages along the way. She called in at Ben's village to say hello. Ben was on duty but Sarah welcomed her with a smile and some cool coconut milk. It tasted delicious. Katie lingered, watching the women sitting cross-legged in a circle. They were busy making a colourful bed-cover. Sarah explained it was a tivaevae. There was a lot of talking and laughing going on. Katie reflected that women all over the world were the same when they got together.

Katie sat with them and fingered the patchwork quilt that symbolised love and friendship. It took many weeks of joint effort to complete one. Katie asked who was getting this one. Sarah told her it was for a distant family member. Katie nodded politely but gave up trying to understand the exact relationship. She left them with their needles, multi-coloured threads and busy tongues, and went on her way.

*　*　*

Farther on down the beach, she met a group of small children she'd played with before. They invited her to join their game of football again, although they didn't think much of her abilities because they put her where she could do the least damage. The enthusiasm and noise of the children made up for her limited ability. She enjoyed herself.

Eventually a smiling mother from the village came to fetch them home. Completely out of breath, Katie waved goodbye, and they disappeared chatting loudly to one another. She threw herself, exhausted, onto the warm silky sand, and the sun dried her skin. There'd soon be a fantastic red and bronze sunset setting the sea aflame.

'I've seen a lot of football games in my time but that one defies description. You're a rotten player. No wonder your side lost.' Daniel's voice cut through the sound of the sea and the wind in the palms.

His voice sent shock waves through her system. She sat up abruptly. He was directly in front of her in damp swimming trunks, a dark blue towel slung around his neck. 'Where did you come from?' she asked.

He tipped his head towards the trunk of a fallen coconut palm. 'I was there watching, in the shade. Your team did their best but they had a very weak defender!'

'I did warn them, but they were kind-hearted because they knew how much I enjoy myself if they let me play.'

They shared a smile.

'If I'd known we had a spectator, I'd have tried harder.'

He looked at her speculatively. 'You like children?'

'Yes I do, very much. Children are honest. You never know where you are with some adults, but children don't waste time on worthless covers-up.' Her feelings were under control again. 'What are you doing on this part of the beach?'

He nodded towards the road. 'I live here. I came down to swim.'

She followed his glance. 'Then your home is well hidden. I can't see it.'

He diverted the conversation. 'It's a long way here from the hotel, isn't it?'

His eyes looked brilliantly blue in his tanned face and she noted the tiny white threads at their outer corners. She was not blind to the attraction of his tanned skin, straight nose, full lips and athletic build. Meeting him on a non-professional level always heightened her awareness. She replied, 'I love strolling along the beach on Sundays. You've lived here all your life and take it all for granted.' She glanced at her watch. 'I won't go any further now though. It'll be dark soon.'

'You must be thirsty after all that racing around. Come up to the house for a drink.'

It was a temptation, but she resisted. 'Thanks, but I won't mess up your weekend.'

He ran his fingers through his hair. 'I realize we're not always on the same wavelength, but there's no reason we can't get on, is there?'

She shrugged.

He asked, 'Have you ever wondered why we're often at odds with each other?'

She pushed her windblown hair out of her face. 'We're both determined and stubborn. You don't like giving in, and neither do I. Clashes are inevitable. It's not worth bothering about.'

'It'd be better if we made an effort to understand each other, wouldn't it?'

'As long as the work is done properly, it doesn't matter if we get on or not, does it?'

'I suppose not, but I'd like us to see eye to eye.'

She tossed her head. 'We do most of the time, especially when you turn on your charm, and I capitulate.'

He threw back his head and laughed. He stretched out his hand and she had no choice. She felt a tingle as their hands met.

He might be a womanizer, a flirt, and someone else's boyfriend, but at this moment he was charming and trying to improve things.

Her main problem was rooted in the fact Paul had made her mistrustful of men and she wanted to keep Daniel out of her personal life. She was wary of relaxing with Daniel. She didn't know if it was because she didn't want to give him the wrong idea, or she was afraid of her own reactions. If they kept their distance there'd be no unasked-for complications. She freed her hand and slapped the sand from her shorts and skimpy top. She managed not to flinch when he brushed the back of her shoulders. She decided this was the wrong time to question why his presence bothered her so much. They fell into step and crossed the road. As they followed the gentle curve of the driveway, the pebbles lurched under her sandals.

When Katie saw Daniel's bungalow, she said impulsively, 'It merges beautifully with the background. I thought you'd want something ultra-modern, but it looks as if it belongs here.'

He smiled and unlocked the door; it opened silently. He turned to her. 'I'm glad you like it. I suggest we sit outside, because at present the air-conditioning is blowing at full power. I'll switch it off and get us something to drink.' He pointed her towards the veranda and left.

Katie leaned against its rail and looked along the island's sunny curves in both directions, and straight ahead at the Pacific Ocean. She remembered Laura telling her about the fabulous views. She was right. There was a modest strip of clear land directly next to the house; otherwise, the area remained wild and overgrown with hibiscus bushes and other tropical greenery.

Daniel had changed into white shorts and a red polo shirt when he returned with a tray. Without asking her what she wanted, he mixed long drinks and handed her one. It tasted delicious.

'What is it? It's very tasty.'

'Pisang Ambong — an Indonesian liqueur with bitter lemon. My mother always liked it.'

She asked politely, 'Does your mother live nearby?' Katie had never heard anyone mention her.

'No. My father died five years ago. She lives in New Zealand.'

'Oh.' She nodded and looked below. 'Laura told me about the wonderful views from here. She was right.' Once it was out, she wished she'd kept her mouth shut.

'Yes. From here, you can watch dolphins fooling around, whales on their way south, all kinds of other marine life, and various kinds of shipping on their way.'

'Have you lived here long?'

'Nearly four years. I always wanted to build here.'

Katie smiled. 'Breakfast on the veranda would be a dream.'

'You're welcome anytime you like.'

She caught her breath and felt her colour rise. She lowered her eyes and concentrated on her glass again. She leaned back into the deep cushions. 'Where do you get your water, and what about drains? Do you do your own housework? Knowing you, you probably don't.'

He threw back his head and laughed. 'You're the first woman to ask those kinds of questions.' He considered her silently for a moment. 'There are large water tanks beneath the bungalow and a large sewage tank. I get it emptied once a year and use it as fertiliser for the plantation.'

Katie wrinkled her nose.

He smiled. 'Yes, it pongs for a couple

of days, but it soon fades away. I manage with one water tank at present but if I ever need more, there are others in position. Usually a couple of downpours in the rainy season fill the main tank. It's also possible to fill them from water trucks in an emergency.'

'I read that the island is volcanic. Wasn't it difficult to dig holes big enough to accommodate tanks?'

'They dynamited the rock and got fast results without damaging the environment. Muriel looks after the place; she lives just down the road. I'm not a messy person by nature. She spends as much time as she needs to keep the place tidy. Sometimes I wonder if it's hers or mine. Like to look around?'

'Yes, of course.' She finished her drink and followed him inside through the French windows.

He showed her around the modern kitchen and comfortable living room before they went down a narrow hallway, past a couple of guestrooms, a bathroom and a home office.

Her sandals echoed on the wooden floors as they went. 'It's super.' When they reached the end of the corridor he threw the last door open with a flourish.

'My personal kingdom.'

Katie walked past him into a spacious bedroom. Panorama windows covered the one wall. Shades of blues and sea-green filled the room. Local paintings in brilliant splashes of colour made an impressive impact. A small veranda provided a perfect patio. She went outside to look. When she returned, she stopped to examine a picture.

He followed her interest. 'I hear you're a bit of an artist yourself.'

'That's a wild exaggeration. I'm not half as good as this.' Curiosity made her ask, 'Who told you that I paint?'

He shrugged and stood with his hands thrust in the pockets of his shorts. 'I don't remember. One of the kitchen staff, I think. You must show me your paintings one day.'

'It'd be a waste of your time. I only paint for fun.'

She looked around again. A beautiful ship in a bottle stood on an antique walnut chest of drawers. Magazines and books covered the top of the bedside table. The soft sunlight sent shafts of light across the cherrywood floor. The king-sized bed dominated the room.

With raised eyebrows, Daniel quipped, 'It's great to lie there and watch the dawn come up, or the stars at night.'

She imagined him there and turned away. 'I'm very, very impressed and I like it. You have a beautiful home. Where's the wardrobe?'

He paused to study her. 'You're unusual, do you know that? There's a walk-in wardrobe through that door, and a connecting en-suite bathroom. Take a look. And give me your approval.'

When Katie returned, she found him standing outside, staring into the distance. Feet wide apart in strong leather sandals, hands thrust into the pockets of his shorts, he looked like master of all he surveyed. He turned and came back through the sliding glass door.

She commented, 'Your wardrobe is huge. You'll never need that much hanging space.'

He flicked her an amused look. 'I will when I get married, won't I? My mother always complained about not having enough room. I remembered that when I built.'

Katie noted that he included marriage in his plans. 'That's true. Women never have enough space for their stuff. The bathroom is beautiful. It's luxury with a big 'L'. I love white bathrooms.'

His eyes twinkled dangerously. 'I'm so glad I chose the right colour. Let's go back outside.'

She followed him, and reflected that his home provided the kind of freedom he needed. Everyone who knew him watched what he did. She sat down and told him about how the women were busy embroidering in Ben's village. 'I've forgotten what Sarah called it. A tiva . . . ?'

'A tivaevae?'

'Yes, exactly. I still don't understand

who's getting it.' She tipped her head to the side. 'Sarah did explain, but she lost me after second cousins, second wives, sister's daughter, or something similar. A real beehive of relations. What's more, she seemed to keep track of everyone. I'd need a computer.'

Daniel began to laugh. 'Don't worry, just nod and pretend you understand. The complexity of island relationships still amazes me, and I grew up here. A tivaevae is very traditional. Tourists would love to buy one but it rarely happens. They take ages to produce. Personally, I'd hate to see them degraded to a machine-made holiday souvenir, but money is a great temptation and I can fully understand that. What about another drink?'

'No, it was delicious but I don't want to stagger back. I try to keep my life private when I'm off duty, but it's not easy. The FBI could learn something from our workers. They want to know everything, and they use sneaky methods if you try to keep quiet.'

He smiled. 'I know what it's like. Why do you think I built this place? You'll survive. I did. There wasn't much alcohol in your drink so you're safe if you'd like another one.'

She stood up. 'No, thanks. I envy you your home. It's like something out of a glossy magazine. You can be proud of it. See you tomorrow?'

He hesitated. 'Katie, you're doing a great job. You've picked up the hotel's management very quickly. I'm sorry if I jump down your throat now and then. I realize how hard you worked to learn everything so fast.'

She was startled. The words almost stuck in her throat, but she got them out. 'That's okay. I love the work. It's even better than I expected because no two days are the same. I like the people in the hotel and I understand why you were scared that I'd mess it all up.' She went towards the veranda steps.

He followed her. A group of orchids with golden-brown blooms grew near the bottom step. He picked one and handed it to her with a flourish.

She lifted it to her nose in confusion. Daniel never ceased to surprise her. 'It's the first time anyone has given me an orchid.'

He raised his brows. 'Really? It won't be the last, I'm sure.'

They saw a taxi coming up the drive. It halted and footsteps crunched on the gravel as Sharon came towards them. When she saw Katie, a fractious expression flitted across her face, but it faded fast.

'Hi Sharon.' Katie could understand if Sharon resented finding another woman with Daniel, but she should trust him. Daniel was too self-assured to stay in love with someone who suffered from jealousy. She said, 'I was walking along the beach and met Daniel. He offered me a drink and a tour of the bungalow. I've never seen it before. It's lovely. I'm just leaving.' She turned to Daniel. 'Thanks!'

He nodded. 'What about a lift? Sharon knows her way around.'

'No thanks. It's not necessary.'

'It'll be dark before you reach the hotel.'

'I'll find it, even in the dark. Bye Sharon.'

Sharon nodded. 'Bye.'

Katie skipped down the steps.

Daniel stood motionless.

Katie hurried off holding the orchid. She looked back from the corner of the bungalow. The two of them were still watching. She waved again. His future wife would get a dream house and an attractive, interesting, and provocative man into the bargain.

She walked home holding on tightly to the orchid.

28

The sunset reflected on the ocean; the surface of the sea looked like a quivering mass of gold. Daniel wished Katie had stayed longer. The more he knew her, the more he liked her. Not just because she worked well, and looked good, but also because she had a decent sense of humour and she used self-confidence to safeguard against intrusion when she thought it was getting too personal. He shook himself free of his thoughts.

Sharon commented, 'I hope that it was her first visit? You know I don't like it one bit.'

He threw his arm around her shoulders. 'Don't get het up about nothing.' He needed to divert her. 'I found those maps showing the original landing places when the first explorers arrived. Want to see them?' He succeeded.

'Very much! Can you still land there by boat?'

Sharon enjoyed sailing and was a good sailor. 'I think so. We can try whenever you have time. Most of them are on quieter parts of the coastline.'

'I'm on duty tomorrow morning. Can we go tomorrow afternoon? My boss believes they won't use boats after all. He thinks they'll use planes instead. It's logical. There's practically no control on the incoming and outgoing flights at the airport.'

He went to get the maps. Most people believed Sharon was a dumb blond. By now, she knew all his friends, all about his previous girlfriends, and the background of most of his employees. People speculated about how serious their relationship was; let them speculate.

29

During the high season, they all worked very hard and there were sometimes lots of problems, but Katie's confidence grew and she didn't need to bother Daniel much anymore. Undoubtedly he did check, but she didn't know how often or when. In her leisure time, Katie joined the people from the hospital when they went out. Her friendship with Judy and Jeff automatically included her in their plans. She was happy to see Jeff and Judy growing closer. They were dating. Katie wondered if they were serious. She didn't ask.

★　★　★

One day, Colin invited her on a sightseeing flight. She met him at his shop and bumped into Laura in the main street.

'Where are you going? Shopping?'

'No, Colin's taking me on a flight around the island. I'm meeting him here.'

Laura's eyebrows lifted. 'Is that plane of his safe?'

'Don't scare me. It's my first trip in a small plane.'

Laura patted her arm and smiled. 'Just a joke! Enjoy yourself.'

Laura had never condemned Colin outright, but Katie knew she didn't like him much and she'd warned Katie to be careful.

When Katie reached his shop, he closed it directly and drove them to the airport. Katie choked an impulse to tell him that closing his shop meant he might lose customers. She already knew he seldom listened to her advice, or anyone else's.

He parked his jeep near the airport fence and greeted someone in dungarees who was repairing his plane. He waved and shouted at someone else working on another aircraft as they passed. Clearly, everyone knew everyone else.

Katie listened to his description as they approached his plane. 'It's a single-engine Cessna. I bought it second-hand from someone who wanted something bigger. One day it'll belong to me and not the bank.'

She noticed someone lounging near the corner of the hangars. He was smoking. Katie thought about the hazard of inflammable substances.

'Know that man? He's smoking! He's looking at us too.'

Colin glanced up and his expression hardened. His scrutiny lasted too long for her to believe him when he said, 'Never seen him before. He's probably looking for a sightseeing flight.' He opened the cabin door with a flourish. 'Let's go. The weather's perfect today.'

Colin helped her in and went around to the other side to hoist himself into the pilot's seat. Once he was settled and wearing headphones, he contacted the tower and started the engine. It sprang to life and ran smoothly. The sight of the propeller so close, and the sound of it spinning round so fast, was exhilarating.

Colin checked with the tower for take-off and steered the plane onto the runway. He revved the engine and, with a roar, the small aircraft picked up speed and took to the sky. She felt breathless as she looked through the windscreen and noticed how fast they left the ground. She looked sideways out of the window. The stranger was still by the hangar. He lifted his hand and saluted.

The Cessna thrust up into the blue. Colin piloted with ease and skill. With butterflies in her stomach, but feeling happy, Katie looked at the buildings dwindling in size as they climbed. Colin was fully concentrating. Katie began to relax and fumbled in her bag for her camera.

When she straightened, the pleasure faded fast. The engine began to run irregularly and sounded rough. Suddenly oil sprayed across the windshield and a haze of smoke began to envelop the cabin. Panic followed a feeling of disbelief. The smoke in the cabin thickened. It bit at her lungs and she began to cough.

Colin uttered through clenched teeth, 'Hold on. We've got to land, fast.'

The engine functioned erratically and spluttered as Colin turned the aircraft sharply towards the runway. They managed to veer around before they began to lose height rapidly. The angle of approach was all wrong even to her untrained eye. Unaware of how dangerous the situation was, Katie knew it wasn't a normal landing. Cowering in her seat in the smoke-filled cabin, she hoped Colin was as good a pilot as he'd always said he was. She closed her eyes and braced her arms against the front panel.

As the plane's wheels hit the runway, a series of challenging bumps shook them. The plane hopped along but Colin managed to keep it on course as they bounced and jostled across the runway. Katie gave thanks for her seat belt. She listened to the fuselage's protests. It remained intact, even though the propeller bit the ground several times. The plane righted itself, dipped, straightened and then carried on. They finally halted, not far from the boundary fence. Through the splotched and blackened windscreen, Katie saw that the propeller blade was completely twisted. They'd survived, but a ghastly silence kept them glued in their seats.

Men shouted and ran towards them with fire-resistant foam, and Colin shouted across at her, 'Get out! Out as fast as you can!'

She wrenched the door open, freed herself from her safety belt, tumbled from her seat and fell into an ungainly heap on the tarmac. On her feet again, one of the men grabbed her. He shoved her in the direction of the buildings. 'Get moving! The engine is overheated; the tank could still explode.'

She ran on shaky legs that somehow functioned. Out of range, she looked back at the activity. The Cessna stood askew, but it wasn't on fire. Colin was in the middle of the bustling action.

Katie was glad to be alone. She walked around the side of a hangar and rested her forehead against the corrugated sheeting. She felt physically sick for a moment, but straightened when she heard a familiar voice.

Daniel had left the door of his car open and the engine running. He charged towards the plane, looking around. When he glanced back and spotted Katie, he spun around and came back at a gallop. He snarled, 'What in God's name were you doing in that plane?' He ruffled his hair. 'Haven't I warned you about him often enough?'

Katie felt shattered. She nodded towards his car. 'You should switch the engine off. This is an airport. There are explosive fumes in the air.'

He glared and went. Afterwards, he wrenched the key from the socket and slammed the door with unnecessary force. She guessed she'd delayed the inevitable, but the temporary breather gave her a minute to rub her palms across her eyes and stifle any impending tears.

His voice lashed out. 'How stupid can you be?'

She said shakily, 'I'm not stupid. It was just bad luck. You're my boss, not my guardian angel. How did you know I was here?' Katie's throat was seizing up and she hoped she'd manage until he left.

'If I did control you, I'd lock you in your bungalow after office hours.' He glowered. 'I met Laura and she told me.' He tipped his head towards the plane. 'She said that you were going up in that thing.'

'There was nothing wrong with the plane until just now.'

'Sure about that? Colin's always short of money. Perhaps he skimped on inspections?'

She hated arguing with him. 'Don't pass judgement on Colin or his plane. You're not a trained mechanic. Or do you have a godly insight about the operative performances of planes?'

His eyes looked dangerous but he replied smoothly, 'I know Colin. I wouldn't trust him further than I can see him. I couldn't care less about him but I'm responsible for you. I don't want to tell your parents you've been killed. That's what nearly happened; do you realize that?'

His words only increased the delayed shock. He rummaged in his pocket while they stared at each other, then handed her his handkerchief. 'Here, wipe your face. It's dirty.'

She snatched it and rubbed her cheeks, then shoved the grubby hand-kerchief back at him. She guessed she looked dirtier than before when she noticed the amusement in his eyes. 'Thanks for your concern, but I'm of age, and I'm just an employee. If I died, I'm sure you'd find a replacement within days.'

Like a bolt out of the blue, he grabbed her. With a furious expression, he crushed her to him and his mouth covered hers hungrily. Despite her anger, his lips felt wonderful. Her stomach whirled and her heart thumped out of control. She prayed he wouldn't notice.

She wanted him, but she didn't trust him, and definitely didn't want a meaningless relationship of short duration. She wanted the love of a lifetime. He attracted her physically, but she needed more than stolen kisses and sex. She pushed him away and rubbed the back of her hand across her mouth. He stared and looked bewildered.

She wanted to be alone so she turned and bolted. She ran without noticing or caring where she went. Once she was out of his sight, the tears tumbled.

★　★　★

Paralysed for a few seconds by something he hadn't reckoned with, Daniel's temper cooled rapidly. He watched Katie's solitary figure vanishing into the distance. By the time he began to react rationally, she'd found a gap in the boundary fence. He watched her scurrying down the empty highway. He ran back to the car and drove out past the entrance for private plane-owners. To his immense irritation, he remembered he'd have to drive around the periphery to reach the spot where she'd been. On the way, he made plans of how he would bundle her into the car and take her back to Rockley. He couldn't. She'd disappeared.

After cruising and checking the side roads, he phoned Laura. She was shocked when Daniel told her what had happened. Laura hadn't seen her. He phoned the hotel. The receptionist told him Miss Warring had arrived by taxi a few minutes ago. She looked dirty and upset and she'd borrowed money from the cash desk to pay for her taxi.

* * *

Colin called to see her at the hotel later that evening. He brought her bag and wanted to check she was okay. They

214

went to the terrace bar. To Katie's surprise, Colin was uptight and edgy. Usually nothing bothered him for long. Perhaps he was worried about finding money for repairs. Emergency cash was non-existent in his vocabulary.

He noticed her inquisitive look and tried to sound bouncy. 'We do end up in bad situations, don't we? Someone has put a voodoo jinx on us. Has Daniel been sticking pins into a doll recently?'

Irritated, she replied, 'That's not funny.'

'Perhaps I should wear a billboard asking, why do these things happen to me?'

'Don't be silly! I'm still suspicious!'

'What about?'

'That man standing by the hangar smoking a cigarette.'

'That's daft.' He played with his glass of beer. 'You do get into tizzies about nothing. I don't know why the crash happened, but why should it have anything to do with a strange man?'

'It's just a feeling.'

'Huh! Just forget it!'

'How can you be so blasé about what happened?'

Colin grinned. 'It's better than worrying all the time. We were damned lucky to get out alive without injuries.'

'I know that, but it doesn't stop me speculating. Is the plane badly damaged?'

'The engine and the undercarriage will need an overhaul. I'm up to date with the insurance coverage, thank God. I'd never knowingly put you in danger, love. I checked the plane yesterday. It was in top condition.'

Katie didn't think she could forget things as easily as he did. Perhaps he was just better at hiding it.

Next morning she wondered if Daniel would lecture her again. She looked up and stiffened momentarily when he arrived.

His face was smooth and blank. If he had intended to say something, he thought better of it and asked, 'How do you feel this morning?'

'I'm fine, thanks.' She paused. 'I

heard you went looking for me.'

He shrugged. 'My anger was focused in the wrong direction. Colin deserved the edge of my tongue, not you.' He smiled and his eyes rested briefly on her mouth.

Katie felt a flurry of goose-pimples and thought he might mention his kiss, but he didn't.

'You were lucky to survive a crash like that without any injury. Friends I talked to convinced me Colin is a better pilot than I thought he was.'

Katie was glad she was off the hook. He held out his hand and she gave him his work for the day.

30

Next day, Colin called to ask Katie out again. She'd already arranged to meet her friends from the hospital. Katie asked him along, hoping he'd fit in. The evening didn't go well. Colin's jokes and repartee didn't work. In fact, he generated several embarrassing moments. She could see that Colin felt awkward. She made an excuse to leave early with him. On their way home, he relaxed and began to banter again.

Even if the others didn't accept him, she was glad of Colin's friendship. Most of the younger people on Naraotoa already had long-standing friendships or they were tourists. You needed time to cultivate real friends and Katie didn't have that much time. She'd made friends with Judy and Laura, but men were more difficult. She enjoyed Jeff's friendship and, although she realized

Colin was unpredictable in other people's eyes, there was something very endearing about his efforts to entertain and amuse her too.

Daniel was the most complicated man she'd met so far, and she thought about him too often. Katie wondered why she hadn't fallen in love with Jeff or Colin, or even stayed with Paul. She recalled Laura's words about not taking second best. Laura was right. Better to remain single than attached to the wrong man.

Jeff and Judy looked happy together. Katie was pleased for them and felt smug when she remembered she'd paired them off in her mind weeks ago.

Next time the crowd from the hospital met, Jeff announced that he'd found a permanent job in New Zealand, in a community hospital not far from Auckland. Everyone cheered and demanded a celebratory round of drinks.

31

Strings of lights decorated the patio, and a large artificial tree with coloured lights stood in the corner of the main lobby.

Judy was going home, Jeff was on duty, and Colin was visiting his parents in Wellington. Katie didn't want to celebrate Christmas on her own, so she was glad when Laura and David invited her to join a group who were getting together on the beach. Daniel and Sharon would be there too.

Laura told her to bring a low-cost gift for a female and something towards the picnic lunch. On Christmas day, when she arrived at the meeting place, Ian was running out to sea. Others lay in untidy groups under the palms. Katie looked up and down the beach. It was busy.

Laura and David gave her a quick

hug and said, 'Merry Christmas!'

'Merry Christmas!' Katie waved to all the others.

Daniel was stretched out on the sand nearby. He looked up, and he smiled for a moment and said, 'Merry Christmas.'

A smile ruffled her mouth when she repeated, 'Merry Christmas' again.

Katie spread her towel in the shade and relaxed. Sharon was playing beach volleyball with a couple of the others. Her bikini showed off her curvaceous figure to perfection and left nothing to the imagination.

Laura sat down. The wind tugged at her beach dress and she tried vainly to drag it back into shape. 'I think you know everyone apart from Sharon's cousin, Gareth. That's him with the red baseball cap.'

Katie nodded and speculated on whether Daniel resented Gareth butting in on his first Christmas with Sharon. Katie swam, and joined in with the games occasionally, after plastering herself with sun cream. People were friendly and included her in the happenings.

Sharon came across once and threw herself down. 'Trying to keep up with the men is gruelling,' she said.

Katie decided there was no reason not to be friendly. 'They're doing it deliberately.' She eyed the male participants. 'They're all machos at heart.'

Sharon's eyes sparkled. 'That's why I love pole-axing them. Come and help!'

'I'd collapse in a matter of minutes and be more of a hindrance than a help in this heat.'

Sharon brushed the loose sand from her legs. 'Don't underrate your abilities. We all break off for a rest now and then. I understand why Daniel likes you.'

Katie's heart missed a beat. 'Does he? We get on most of the time, but we quibble a lot too.'

Sharon studied her. 'You have more in common than you think.' Then Gareth shouted to her and she galloped off again.

* * *

The picnic lunch was delicious, and laughter and comments accompanied every dip into the present sack. Katie drew a red-and-white sarong.

Daniel hid his present after he'd opened it. He turned his back on everyone.

Ian was too curious. 'Aw, come on! What did you get?'

At last, laughing, he waved a copy of Playboy with a near-naked blonde posed next to a Christmas tree. The men crowded around to look and then Ian grabbed it. The boys ran off and began to squeal loudly as they turned the pages.

Laura looked on disapprovingly.

Ian shouted, 'You'll get it back, eventually.'

Everybody capitulated to the heat. He, or she, was soon lying higgledy-piggledy fashion in the shade underneath the palm trees in the warm wind. Katie watched them from behind her sunglasses, and studied Daniel.

Someone close by was trying to sing a Christmas carol. She thought about her family. They'd be together today, eating turkey and wearing paper hats. She got up and slipped quietly away. Out of reach, she donned a long T-shirt and slapped a straw hat on her head. She walked parallel with the waves. The air was cooler, and she found a grove of mangroves around the bend. She straddled one of the thicker intertwining aerial roots, dangled her feet in the clear water, and was glad of the shade. She was there when David joined her.

'I saw you leaving. Mind if I join you?'

'No, of course not. Is Laura sleeping?'

'Like a log. This is a nice spot. There's a breeze coming in from the sea.'

She nodded, but remained silent.

'Is everything all right, Katie? Too much sun?'

'No, I was thinking about home.' She had no inhibitions talking to David and added, 'I miss them all. I've missed the excitement of my sister's pregnancy. She wasn't even pregnant when I left, and the baby will be born before I get back.'

'I'm sure they're thinking about you too. That plane accident has probably heightened your senses of family and belonging, even though you got off scot-free.'

She smiled at him. 'Yes, we were lucky, weren't we?' She switched subjects. 'Why aren't you tired?'

'I just can't keep up with all the non-stop sporting activity anymore, so I try to avoid it. That means I'm not as tired as some of the others are. I did wonder if Daniel had jumped on your toes again.'

'Why?'

'Much to my amazement, when your name cropped up the other day he actually admitted that he hasn't always been fair to you.'

'We weren't always on the same wavelength, but he's well-behaved most of the time now.'

David's eyes twinkled. 'Then watch out. He'll probably pounce again any day now.'

She chuckled. 'Yes, he's not very predictable, is he?' She paused. 'Perhaps Sharon will have a steadying effect.'

'I hope not. I've always liked him because he sticks to his guns, and because what he says and does is sometimes too radical for some people.'

Katie decided David didn't yet know how much Sharon already influenced Daniel. She'd seen it.

The two of them walked back and the seawater played with their feet. There were dark shapes under the palms everywhere, but not everyone slept. Katie saw Daniel coming towards them. His sports shirt flapped around his evenly bronzed chest. He looked like a Greek god.

When they met, he remarked, 'I wondered where you two were.'

'We were back there, among the

mangroves,' David answered.

Katie was confident enough to tuck her arm through David's. 'Yes, I had this attractive doctor all to myself. Laura is a very lucky woman. David, do you have an eligible twin brother?'

'If I did, I can't think of anyone else I'd like more as a sister-in-law.'

Daniel eyed them and grinned. 'I see! I've stumbled on a mutual admiration society, haven't I?'

David clapped him on his shoulder. 'Why, are you jealous, old man?'

Daniel raised his eyebrows. 'I'll give you a friendly warning, Katherine Warring. This man's wife is a hellcat when she's jealous.'

Katie frowned. 'In that case, I'd better be careful! I don't fancy a confrontation with Laura.' She moved away from them towards the crest of the sand, to walk underneath the shadows of the palms while the men continued to stroll along the water's edge together.

Katie's thoughts wandered and she wondered why she wanted to be in

Daniel's company so much. Sharon had a right to him; she didn't. She came to an abrupt halt and felt totally bewildered when she realized she'd fallen in love with him.

For a moment, the world stood still and she took a deep breath. Feeling confused, and her thoughts in turmoil, she forced herself to continue. When she reached the others, some were still sleeping. She was glad to have time to adjust.

Falling in love with Daniel was stupid, but could she have prevented it happening? She'd started out almost disliking him, but that hadn't stopped her interest continually growing. She was certain it was love because what she felt for Daniel had no comparison to what she thought she'd felt for Paul. Daniel only needed to be near and her whole being came alive. He had tunnelled his way into her heart and he was the other half she'd always searched for. She stared into the distance and saw Sharon running towards the sea. Daniel was destined for someone else. She needed to distract her thoughts and went to talk to Laura.

'Where's David? Not another emergency at the hospital, I hope?'

Katie shook her head. 'He's with Daniel.'

When the two men returned, Katie willed herself not to look at Daniel.

The peak of activities had passed. Soon after some more feeble attempts to prolong things, the beach party ended. Everyone was tired. Laura struggled up the banking towards their car and called back, 'Katie, how are you getting back to the hotel?'

The Stannards' car would be full with Ian and his friends. Katie waved. 'I'm fine. It's all organized.'

Laura assumed what Katie intended and waved again before carrying on.

'Who's giving you a lift?' Daniel's voice cut in over her shoulder.

'No one. I'm going to walk, but don't tell Laura that. She'll feel obliged to organize something.'

'Don't be silly. You can come with me.'

She lowered her gaze. 'Have you room?'

'An empty car. Is that room enough?'

'What about your friends?' She couldn't bring herself to mention Sharon's name.

'Sharon intends to end the day in her hotel bar. I'm going home. Stop fishing around for excuses; come on.'

Katie followed him. There'd be time to think sensibly later, back in her room. He threw her bag onto the back seat.

'What happened to your present?' she quipped.

He smirked. 'It's probably a write-off and I didn't even see it properly.'

She chuckled. 'If you're that interested, buy a new one.'

They were approaching Rockley, but he drove straight past and explained, 'David told me you were down in the mouth. I'll drive you home later.'

She felt self-conscious 'I missed my family but I'm perfectly okay now. You don't need to entertain me.'

'Katie, I wasn't planning anything special. If you're there, or not, it won't change my plans.'

She gave in.

'I presumed you'd be with Jeff, or even my favourite guy of all time, Colin.'

Katie shook her head. 'Jeff is on duty over Christmas and anyway, he and Judy are going steady.'

'And Colin?'

'He's visiting his parents in Wellington. I'm not hunting for a boyfriend, Daniel! I don't need emotional ties; I'll be leaving soon.'

'Some people who come here stay forever.'

'Not many. The South Sea fascination wears off unless you have a job to keep you busy. I met an Englishman recently who told me he had to do something, or go mad. He started an orchid farm. It's different for you; you've grown up here.'

They'd reached their destination. Katie got out and hooked her bag. Daniel unlocked the door and held it open.

32

'I'm taking a shower. What about you?' Daniel said.

'Not much point. I don't have any fresh clothes.'

'Hmm!' Katie's stomach knotted as Daniel's investigating stare moved from top to bottom. 'I've a T-shirt that's shrunk in the wash,' he told her. 'You can wear that with your new sarong. To save me facing complicated explanations and Muriel's sharp tongue, it'd be helpful if we used the same shower.'

Katie stared in disbelief. 'You'd pounce on any cleaner like a ton of bricks if they tried to order you about at the hotel. I don't believe this!'

He looked sheepish. 'You haven't met Muriel.'

Katie decided that Muriel must be worth meeting.

He whistled and went. Katie felt

extraordinarily happy. This evening was so special, knowing she was here with him, in his home. Ten minutes later he was back. He gestured her down the corridor. 'Off you go. There's a fresh towel, and the T-shirt is on the bed.' He added, tongue in cheek, 'It's white, so it won't clash.'

She felt like a bottle of champagne about to pop. In his bedroom, she ran her fingers over the ship in the bottle and picked up a paperback lying face-down on the bedside table. The view of the evening sky took her breath away. Lying in that bed watching the sun rise or the stars come out must be awesome. She shook herself; he'd wonder why she was taking so long.

She managed to wrap the sarong quite expertly; she'd practised with the one Sarah gave her. The T-shirt flapped until she tied it in a large knot on the side. Looking in the mirror, she was satisfied. She tidied the bathroom and padded barefoot back down the corridor.

Daniel called before she reached the living room. He handed her the telephone. 'For you.'

'No one knows I'm here. What's wrong? The hotel? Hello!' When she heard her mother answer, she was stunned for a second or two.

'Hello, Katie. Merry Christmas, love! How are you? What are you doing? Dad and I were just reminiscing about how we've always been together at Christmas. This is the first time without you, and we miss you.'

Katie pulled herself together. 'I miss you too. I've been on the beach with friends. Mr. McCulloch has invited me this evening, so I'm not alone. How's Sara? And Dad?'

'Sara is fine. So is Dad; he's standing next to me. He sends his love, and your brother-in-law is poking me in the ribs to send you their love too. Just being able to hear your voice has made my day.'

Crackling began to interrupt them. Katie rushed on. 'Marvellous to hear your voice, Mum. I'll write soon. Enjoy Christmas. Love to everyone I know. Bye!' She heard 'Bye Katie' before the sound died. She moved towards the activity in the kitchen. 'Daniel, how can I thank you?'

He stood with two long-stemmed crystal glasses dangling between the fingers of one hand. He surveyed her, eyebrows raised. 'Feel better?'

She nodded. 'I thought about phoning, but the ordinary telephone connections are nearly always bad. I intended to try this evening.'

'I asked Joyce to let me jump the queue. I know her. Our old-fashioned telephone exchange still functions, but the island needs to invest in a better satellite reception and get up to date. I'll bring it up at the next meeting of the island's administration. You already know how unpredictable the internet connection is.'

She nodded. 'Yes. It's very annoying, especially when it's important. I've given up trying to talk to them via

Skype. The connection is always lousy. How did you know my parents' number?'

'From the application form you sent to the agency. I've opened a bottle of champagne to celebrate Christmas.' He handed her a glass. 'Here's to Christmas all over the world, to loved ones near and far, and to us.'

She mused briefly that the employment agency must have sent him all the details after all, so he knew all about her working qualification and why they sent her. She sipped the golden liquid and decided that he was a terrific man.

'Hungry? I've some salad, cold chicken, and cheese in the fridge. By the way, that outfit is very becoming.'

She relished the compliment. 'No, I'm not hungry, thanks, but you go ahead.'

'Sure?' He piled some chicken legs onto a plate, grabbed a paper serviette, and led the way back to the living room.

'Your mother lives in New Zealand. Doesn't she ever come to share your

Christmas?' She put her hand to her mouth. 'Sorry! It's none of my business.' Katie watched him pulling the meat off the drumsticks with his strong teeth.

He waved a half-eaten one and shook his head. 'She knows Christmas is a busy time at the plantation. My uncle lives near her so she's never alone. This island harbours too many memories of my father. Perhaps she'll visit again one day. We get on, apart from her never-ending hints that it's time for me to get married and give her some grandchildren.'

'Any siblings?'

'Unfortunately, no. She worries about me as if I'm still six years old. I visit her as often as time allows.'

'Where did you go to university?' She could question him without it arousing too much suspicion today.

'In Dunedin.' He sucked his fingers and wiped his hands on a paper serviette.

'What did you study?'

'Economics and history. I enjoyed

New Zealand very much. It's a beautiful country with friendly people. Like something else to drink?'

'No, this is fine. You took the perfect subjects for a business career.'

'A degree helps, but it doesn't guarantee success. You need drive and determination. My father also financed my beginnings and that makes a huge difference. Persuading a bank manager to back you is very hard these days.'

'Did you know about how to run a hotel before you started?'

'I earned pocket money in the vacations and I took a management course before I built Rockley. When it was financially viable, I brought Marjorie in to run it, because I needed more time to run other things by then. I like new challenges. I provide work for people, and enjoy a good personal lifestyle. What more can anyone want?'

'You never wanted to live anywhere else?'

'No. I like the people here, and the sun.' He leaned forward and put the plate on the table. 'You're adventurous too, otherwise you wouldn't be here today.'

'Yes, I enjoy meeting people and I love the work. The island is a dream come true. I think I'd almost consider working here for nothing.' She saw the amusement in his eyes.

'Naraotoa isn't the paradise you think it is. There's corruption and a darker side to the island. Kids get into trouble here like anywhere else in the world. There are tricksters, thugs and criminals here too.'

'Yes, I know that, but you don't see the problems unless you're directly involved, do you?'

'What are your plans when you return home? What about your old job?'

'My old company went bust. My parents will keep an eye on adverts so that I can apply from here.'

'Look, the sun is about to disappear. Let's go watch!'

She followed him onto the veranda. They sat and talked about recent news on the radio and TV.

A frangipani tree grew at the side of the veranda. The long, tapering stems had reddish-purple clusters of flowers and the perfume filled the night air. It was blooming all over the island in a multitude of different colours at the moment. Katie tossed the liquid around her glass. 'I wonder where the name frangipani comes from.'

'I looked it up. Apparently, a Marquis Frangipani created a perfume used to scent gloves in the 16th century. Catherine de Medici used it.' He looked across and added, 'Another Katie! When people on voyages of discovery found the frangipani flower, its perfume reminded them of that other perfume, and they gave it his name.'

'What a brilliant way to be remembered.' They sat together watching the sun sliding out of sight in a blaze of red and gold. Katie was very conscious that Daniel seemed to be someone who enjoyed the same things as she did.

'How does your family usually celebrate Christmas Day?' he asked her.

'We eat too much, exchange presents, and laze around. We sometimes go for an afternoon walk, if there's snow on the ground.'

'And in the evening?'

'We usually play charades; do you know what I mean?' He nodded. 'Or Monopoly, because my dad thinks he's a world champion.'

'Charades won't work with just the two of us, and I can't offer snow, but I'll have a go at Monopoly if you like.'

She tilted her head to the side and said, 'Really?'

'I think I still have the game somewhere. We played it often too.' He ruffled through a cupboard noisily and emerged triumphantly with a battered box.

In the end, after a game filled with laughter and protests, he emerged as the winner with Katie owing him twenty thousand dollars. They were like two friends spending time together, not at all like a boss and his employee.

He indicated to her glass. 'Like some more?'

'No thanks.' She looked at her watch. 'I'd better go. Thanks for a lovely evening, Daniel. I really enjoyed it. Will you please now be the perfect host and drive me home? If you're tired, I can walk back; it won't take me long and it's quite safe.'

He unfurled his long frame and stood up. 'No, I'll drive you home. I only had one glass of champagne, ages ago.' He quipped, 'I hoped we could share breakfast on the veranda.'

He probably said the same to every woman. 'What about your T-shirt?' she asked.

'Keep it. It doesn't fit me anymore.'

★ ★ ★

The journey whizzed by. 'Thanks, and goodnight!' She kissed his cheek quickly before she got out.

Katie noted how startled he looked. Curse it! She'd given in to temptation. She walked away quickly without looking back.

33

The restaurant was fully booked for the hotel's New Year celebrations.

Laura and David invited Katie to their party, but she turned them down. If she worked, someone else would be free. Jeff and Judy also asked her along to a party that the younger members of the hospital were organizing, but Katie refused that too. Some people, like the kitchen staff, were always working when others were enjoying themselves. She had no idea where Daniel would be and didn't ask.

As the hotel New Year's Eve party got underway, the sounds of festivity from the terrace got louder and noisier. They drifted indoors to Katie in reception. The hands of the clock crept towards midnight. With a few minutes to go, Lesperon came from the kitchen and dragged her out to the terrace to join the mass of boisterous guests and staff.

The fun and laughter was infectious. Everyone waited as the last minute of the old year ticked away. With seconds to go, Lesperon dashed off to get them something to drink.

Someone put a glass of champagne in her hand and suddenly Daniel was there. She stopped breathing for a moment. Dressed more formally than usual, in a midnight-blue suit and matching tie, she wondered why he'd left his party to come here. Someone counted the last seconds of the year. Ten, nine, eight . . . three, two, one, zero. A booming 'Happy New Year' rang through the air.

Among the cheers and commotion, Daniel said, 'Happy New Year, Katie Warring.'

'Happy New Year, Daniel McCulloch.' He bent his head and brushed her lips gently with his. It sent the pit of her stomach into a wild swirl. They surveyed each other silently, amid the chaos and noise around them. His eyes made her pulses race. 'Auld Lang Syne' played and people stood singing and dancing. Daniel took Katie's glass and put it on the nearest table and then took her into his arms, and they moved slowly among the milling masses.

With her head against his shoulder, she clung to him, one hand hugging his neck. Her hair brushed his chin. The music grew louder and faster again. He released her and somehow she managed to remark. 'I thought you'd be celebrating with your friends.'

He guided her to the outer edge. It gave Katie time to get her feelings under control again.

'I think lots of my friends are here, aren't they? I wanted to check everything was okay. In the past, people sometimes went crazy and caused a lot of damage.' He looked around. 'No oddballs this time though.'

'No, so far it's been pure fun. Someone told me a visitor from New Zealand did try to climb the coconut palm next to the bar to put up the New Zealand flag, but he fell off. Luckily, he didn't hurt himself.' She eyed the merriment. 'I wonder how long the party will last.'

'Till they all fall over, I expect. We usually find a variety of bodies stretched out on the beach on New Year's morning. Why didn't you go to Laura's party?'

She shrugged. 'I decided to give someone else a break.'

'Do you want to continue with the fun?'

She shook her head. 'No, not really.'

'Then grab a glass of champagne on the way and enjoy a good night's sleep.' He gave her a gentle push. 'I'll check things before I leave. Off you go.'

Katie presumed that he was returning to Sharon. If she'd been Daniel's girlfriend, she'd have made sure she was with him at the stroke of midnight.

34

Jeff gave a farewell party. A small crowd, mostly from the hospital, were already there when Katie arrived. David and Laura were across the room and she waved. Eventually, she got close enough to wish Jeff luck.

'I hope you like your new job.'

'Thanks, Katie.'

'Let me know how you get on.'

'I'm not much of a letter-writer. I'll try.'

'Then my only real hope is Judy.'

He smiled. 'You'll be leaving soon yourself. When?'

'In a couple of weeks. I'll miss you both. Judy has been a good friend. I like her very much.'

He tilted his head and his eyes sparkled. 'And so do I! She's special.'

★ ★ ★

When she cornered Judy, Katie said, 'I'm really happy for you. Jeff just mentioned you're thinking of following him to New Zealand?'

'I've already put in my notice.'

Katie's eyebrows lifted.

'I decided this week. I applied for a new job Christmas-time, but even if I don't get that one, I've decided to go back to New Zealand anyway.' Judy's eyes searched the crowd. It was clear that she and Jeff had found what everyone hoped to find one day.

Katie eventually came across David and Laura among the throng of people too. She invited them out for a meal. It was the nearest she could get to entertaining them, and she was grateful for their friendship.

35

The most hectic part of the year was over, although the hotel was still very busy. Katie discovered that Daniel gave his annual party at this time of year, and people were anxious to get an invitation.

One morning Daniel handed her a list of names. 'Make me an invite for Saturday the twentieth, please.'

She did. The dog-eared telephone directory, and Ben, solved the problem of finding the right addresses. Daniel signed them and delivered several personally to the members of the staff. Apparently, he rotated who got one every year. Katie noticed her name wasn't included.

An invitation to a Buckingham Palace garden party couldn't have caused more fuss.

Katie and Laura played golf as usual

on Thursday. They shared a drink afterwards. 'I wish I'd kept something special to wear,' Laura said. 'I forgot all about Daniel's party. I saw a fabulous dress with a draped bodice in a fashion magazine last week. The dressmaker on Wallace Street is awfully clever. Give her a picture and the right material, and she'll produce a copy in no time at all. She's an artist with a needle. You should try her.'

Katie nodded but didn't comment. She wouldn't be around much longer to worry about new dresses. Laura left in a rush with, 'See you Saturday.' Katie didn't have time to tell her she wouldn't be there.

She spent a leisurely Saturday. After her evening meal, she went to her room. She'd planned to send her sister an email but she couldn't concentrate, so she picked up a bundle of blouses and went to the laundry instead.

She switched on a small radio standing on the shelf and listened to hits from the eighties. It made a boring job more bearable.

'Hi, Katie.'

She looked up and saw Daniel leaning against the doorframe, his car keys jingling in his hand. Whenever he appeared suddenly, like now, she had to struggle with her feelings and try to mask her face. She smiled hesitatingly. 'What are you doing here? Forgotten something for the party?'

'Umm! Vodka. I slipped away to raid the hotel bar. I noticed the lights when passing. Doing something important?' He glanced at her ironing. 'Aren't you coming?

'No.'

'Why not?'

'I wasn't invited.'

He looked baffled. 'What do you mean? Of course you're invited.'

'You never said so.'

He paused. 'I presumed you knew that you were. I took too much for granted again, didn't I? I do want you to come. Come back with me now.'

'I'm not dressed for a party.'

'You look fine; you always do. I'll get the vodka and meet you outside in five minutes.'

She wanted to go so she just nodded. She would have chosen something more festive than the lightweight jeans dress, but there wasn't enough time to change. She went as she was. Sharing Daniel with dozens of people at his party was better than nothing. It was another memory for the empty years ahead.

He manoeuvred the car into an empty space. Festoons of party lights decorated the carport and some people were already dancing there. Daniel said hello to someone, reached for Katie's hand, and pulled her along inside.

The room was packed. Daniel fought his way through the throng to one of the corners. He left Katie with David and Laura. 'Get Katie something to drink, will you, David? I've got to find Howard.' He gave her a nod and disappeared.

'Where've you been?' Laura hissed. 'You're late.'

Lengthy explanations were pointless. Katie looked around. 'In this crowd, I don't think my presence matters. I'm not even an islander.'

One of Laura and David's friends, Rob, asked her to dance. His wife warned Katie, 'He thinks he's Fred Astaire but he's more like a whirling dervish.'

Katie tried to keep up with him and almost failed. The sweat poured down his face. He certainly knew how to enjoy himself and smiled expressively when they returned to the others.

'Well?' His wife looked at Katie sympathetically.

Rob was in high spirits. 'With a bit of practice, Katie and I could win competitions.'

His wife commented, 'If you don't get a heart attack in the process!'

Laura tried to sound annoyed when she told them about Ian. 'From his last letter, he spends more time enjoying himself than studying.'

Katie knew just how proud Laura

was of Ian. 'Not long ago you told me he was working too hard. Ian knows what he's doing. Don't be such a fussy hen.'

She spotted Daniel in the crowd with people clustered around him. He was outspoken, unpredictable, and no ordinary man. He was special. She ignored thoughts about next month or next year. She'd have to face the future without him, but not now. Eventually Daniel joined them and was clearly satisfied that everything was humming.

Rob said, 'I'm thinking about making a ship in a bottle. I found a book about how to do it in the church jumble sale. I'll try something simple first. I remember your father had a beautiful one, didn't he, Daniel?'

Daniel paused and, not stopping to think, Katie exclaimed, 'You mean the one in his bedroom? It's amazing, isn't it?'

Glances flew back and forth and the ensuing hush put her face to flame.

Daniel's expression remained bland,

but his mouth twitched. 'Yes, it certainly is. It's a model of a trader that sailed between Jakarta and Holland in the last century. You can borrow it if you like, but you'll need to learn a lot before you'll manage anything half as good.'

Laura's eyebrows were halfway up her forehead, and her mouth was slightly open. Unspoken questions were written in her eyes. David waved unnecessarily at someone on the other side of the room. The conversation picked up again and Katie longed to sink through the floor. She guessed what they were thinking. After a few minutes of trying to avoid questioning looks, she backed away into the crowd.

She kicked herself for her stupidity. Sharon would skin Daniel alive if anyone mentioned it to her. There wasn't any point in trying to clear things tonight; they'd only be more suspicious. She'd tell Laura the facts next time they met, and leave it up to her to spread the truth.

She went outside and skirted Ben and his wife dancing energetically among other people in the crowded carport. She walked the length of the bungalow, dodging the vegetation on the way. The music had faded by the time she reached the veranda outside his bedroom. She sat on the steps. Gradually, her eyes adjusted to the gloom.

She heard the sliding door swish softly. Katie looked back. Daniel held onto the doorframe, his legs crossed casually at the ankles. 'My, oh my! You've given them food for thought for a while.'

She snapped, 'Go away! You could've explained that I only saw the ship by chance.'

He gave a throaty laugh. His face was shrouded by the shadows. 'Do you honestly think they'd believe me? You put your foot in it, not me.'

'I know. That's why I'm mad. I'm now branded as a blatant trollop who's having a clandestine affair with my boss.'

'Oh, forget it, Katie. Let them think what they like. Does it matter? This is the twenty-first century. Most of them won't give it a second thought.'

'Laura will. I'll face the Spanish Inquisition next Thursday when we meet for golf.'

He chortled. 'Consider it to be a feather in your cap! They know Marjorie never ensnared me in the bedroom. Oh, come on. Ignore the tittle-tattle, gossip, and the rumours. I have to, all the time.'

'Go away! You make me feel worse, not better. What about Sharon? If someone tells her, she won't ask when and why, and you'll be up the creek.'

'Let me worry about Sharon. You can't hide for the rest of the evening. That'll confirm your guilt! It's not very flattering that you're annoyed just because people believe we're having an affair.'

'You don't need flattery from me. You're used to leaving broken hearts along the way.' Katie stopped. She wished she'd bitten off her tongue. 'I'm sorry. That's rude. I shouldn't listen to tittle-tattle, should I?'

'No! Truth is flexible; it depends on who's giving, and who's receiving, it.' He held out his hand and pulled her up. His fingers brushed her cheek. She turned away and he followed her back around the house. The sounds of laughter and music filled the air again. When they parted in the carport, his eyes were full of laughter. She stayed there and joined the crowd with Ben and Sarah.

Katie walked home with the others as far as their village. All of them were happy and slightly inebriated. Katie carried on with one of the maids who lived in the hotel. The ocean was a myriad of silver moonbeams rippling the surface. The night air was full of the South Pacific. It was almost too good to waste in sleeping.

Next morning, she'd never been more reluctant to leave the realm of dreams. After a late breakfast, she considered phoning Daniel to ask if he needed help to clear up the aftermath of the party. After some soul-searching, she decided not to. That was Sharon's job, not hers.

Katie faced Laura resolutely when they met. Laura referred to the ship in the bottle straight away. 'Is something going on between you two? I thought he wasn't your cup of tea? What about Sharon?'

'I met Daniel on the beach one Sunday and he offered me a drink and showed me round the bungalow. That's when I saw the ship in the bottle. I knew you'd misunderstood, but I couldn't explain fast enough, and Daniel didn't help either.'

'Oh! I see. I'm glad. I like Daniel but I don't want you to get hurt.'

36

Daniel hesitated on his way out. His eyes froze on Katie's long, lean form and he caught her by surprise when he asked, 'What are you doing tomorrow?'

'Me? I don't know yet. Why?'

'Like to come sailing with me to one of the outer islands?'

Katie hoped she looked a lot calmer than she felt. 'Yes, I'd like that very much. Judy told me how much she enjoyed herself.'

He looked pleased. 'Good. Is seven thirty too early? I'll pick you up.'

'No. That's fine.'

'We'll make a day of it.'

She felt a warm glow. 'I'll bring something to eat.'

His eyes showed his satisfaction. 'Til tomorrow then?'

She nodded. After he'd left, Katie wanted to cheer.

*　*　*

She asked Lesperon to provide picnic food.

'Where are you going, Katie? Who's going with you?'

'Daniel's taking some people out on his yacht and he asked me along.'

He grinned. 'Ooh-la-la! You've heard about the boss's reputation I hope?'

She laughed. 'Daniel already has a girlfriend.'

*　*　*

She avoided the lobby and walked down the driveway. She wore a bikini under white trousers, and a black-and-white T-shirt. She sat down on a bordering stone. Daniel drew up and she brushed the seat of her trousers before picking up the basket.

'You're on time. Why are you waiting here?' he said.

'Because I haven't a life of my own.' She held on to her straw hat as the

261

wind tried to snatch it away."

'So you sneaked out? If you acted like a tyrant, they'd leave you alone. They like you and think they're entitled to know.'

They drifted into a comfortable silence and she relaxed.

He parked in a shady corner near the jetty. Lifting the basket, he asked, 'Good heavens! What's in here?'

'Just bits of this and that.'

They looked at each other and smiled. 'Let's go on board,' Daniel said. 'It's still quiet, so we'll be one of the first out beyond the reef this morning.'

Katie followed him until he stopped in front of a sleek white yacht bobbing up and down in the water. 'It's very impressive and bigger than I expected.'

'Do you know anything about boats?'

'No, nothing. It's the first time for me to be on a yacht.'

He looked at her plimsolls. 'Well, you're wearing the right shoes,' he hinted. 'People walk barefoot on board but you'll need them to go ashore.

Coral reefs are sharp underfoot.'

She took them off and he handed her aboard. Bare-footed, she soon found her sense of balance. She wondered where the others were.

'Take the basket down to the galley. I'll deal with the mooring lines.'

'Where are the others?'

'Others? Who exactly?' He shoved the peak of his cap further up his forehead.

'Sharon for a start.'

Annoyance flitted across his face. 'Sharon's working. Want to change your mind?'

Startled, she murmured, 'No, of course not.' She stared at him and cleared her throat. 'Need any help? If you think I can do something useful, just tell me.'

His expression softened. 'We'll use the engine until we're beyond the outer reef. If the wind is strong enough, I'll put you at the helm when I hoist the sails.'

'Are you properly insured?'

Her heart thumped madly when she went below. Dumbfounded, she leaned against the shiny woodwork. She barely noticed her surroundings. If she'd known they'd be alone, she wouldn't have come, but it was too late now. Worrying wouldn't help. She glanced around at the surroundings and jumped when he called.

She put the bottles in the fridge and left the rest in the basket. She took a deep breath. Perhaps he wanted to give her a day out on his yacht because she was leaving soon. Once they cleared the reef, he increased speed and headed out to sea. She sat down on the leather seat behind the wheel. She closed her eyes and lifted her face to the sun. She commented, 'I expected you to have a kind of narrow racing yacht. This is much bigger than I expected.'

He glanced back briefly. 'I opted for this one because it's fast, and big enough for four adults to sleep on board.'

She looked up at the sky. 'Do you

realize that you're working hard and I'm lazing? In less than a year your manager has made fantastic progress!'

'I'm earning my share of the food; otherwise you'll probably keep it all to yourself.'

'Think I could be that niggardly?'

His eyes danced. 'Yes.'

'How do you know where you're going?'

'Experience. I've sailed since I was a kid. I use charts, or satellite navigation if I'm in doubt.'

The waves grew choppier, but it was exhilarating. He held course, despite the wind's efforts to push them astray. Her clothes were plastered to her body like a second skin.

He looked up. 'If you take the wheel, I'll hoist the main sail and we'll make more speed.'

'What if I can't stay in control?'

'I'll throw you overboard into shark-infested waters, so hold on tight. You only have to stop the wheel spinning.'

She felt ridiculously happy and

watched him hoist the sail and position it across the boat so that the wind coming from behind drove them along even faster. They skimmed across the water. He took the wheel again and Katie noted she felt more comfortable with him than anyone she'd ever met before.

'Coffee? That's the crew's job,' he said.

'And if I refuse?'

'I told you before — the ocean is full of hungry sharks!'

'In that case, coffee coming up, sir.'

The coffee tasted wonderful and time passed quickly.

Daniel pointed to a small dark spot straight ahead. 'That's our destination.'

Minutes later, he lowered the sail and used the motor to guide the boat between the dark coral reefs into the quiet safety of a natural bay. Sometimes the hull and the side of the reef looked centimetres apart. Katie watched in fascination. He anchored and stretched his body towards the sun.

'Let's make the most of the day. I'll take the basket. The water reaches my chin here so I'm afraid you'll have to swim, walk underwater, or wait until I come back to fetch you.'

'I'll swim.' She took off her T-shirt and trousers and left them down in the cabin.

Daniel undressed down to his swimming trunks and Katie secretly admired his long, muscled body. She fetched the picnic basket from below, and added her camera.

'Remember to wear your shoes. I'll go first.' He dived off neatly over the side, and reappeared immediately. Water trickled down his face. She handed him the basket and he waded toward the beach. She slipped over the side, held on to some rope and pushed off. She caught up with him and they walked up the beach.

She looked around. Coconut palms lined the fringes of the beach and dark coral bordered the edges of the bluish-green water. 'What's it called?'

'Paradise Lost. There's no fresh water here apart from the occasional rain shower. It's amazing that any plants survive. Follow me! There's a sheltered cove round the next bend.'

She took her camera from the basket and took a picture of the yacht at anchor. Daniel waited. She turned to take a picture of him. He put up his hand to protest.

'It's only a souvenir photo for me.'

'Only if you use the self-timer, and join me.'

Katie positioned the camera and ran to him. Laughing, he draped his arms around her. The camera clicked. Katie hid her reactions and retrieved the camera. The photo might be the only one she'd ever have of them together. He took them around the bend and the overhanging rocks. The next bay was quieter and more sheltered from the wind. Katie looked around with plea-sure. 'Let's explore. How big is the island?'

He groaned. 'Can we eat first?'

She tilted her head to the side. 'Only if you're very hungry.'

'I am. My breakfast was non-existent.'

She unpacked the food and gestured. 'There, help yourself.'

She relished sharing their meal. He suggested they save the wine and fruit for later.

Katie looked around in contentment. 'This really is a bit like paradise.'

'I'm ready to show you around now.' He pulled her up. They took their time and walked in the shade whenever possible. They found a dilapidated hut with a missing roof and palm-leaf walls. The door hung haphazardly. There were the remains of a fire in the centre of the hardened floor, and a broken saucepan lay on its side near one of the walls.

'Fishermen probably use it as a stop-over,' Daniel said.

'Have you ever stayed here over-night?'

'Mmm! Often! A sleeping-bag on the beach and a sky full of stars is better than any five-star hotel.'

They went on. Even Katie could tell the island couldn't support long-term habitation. Water was non-existent. 'Think anyone will ever live here permanently?'

'Shouldn't think so. Running a de-salting machine would cost the earth. You'd also get bored to death with nothing to do.'

'Who owns it?'

'As far as I know the government. Someone applied to build a luxury hideaway once, but it was turned down. I'm glad. It wouldn't have produced any long-term jobs.'

'I'm glad too. It's perfect as it is.'

He nodded. 'Let's go back to the cove.'

37

They clambered over rocks, past over-hanging vegetation, down slopes and along the shell beaches. Sometimes their arms or hands touched as he helped her along. Katie's emotions were at an all-time high.

When they reached the cove again, they went for a swim. Katie didn't go far out before she turned for the shore again. Daniel noticed and swam back to join her. He flopped down, the sea water dripping from his face and body. Life seemed perfect.

'A glass of wine?' His voice cut into her thoughts.

'Yes, a great idea.'

Passing her a half-filled glass, he took a generous sip of his own. 'Nectar for the gods.'

'Today is perfect. I'll always remember it.' She lifted her glass.

He toasted her glass and took a sip. Their eyes met and their knuckles touched. Her heart thumped at an awesome pace. Silence ruled, apart from the sound of the sea hitting the coral reefs. Holding her gaze, he leaned forward took her glass and ran a finger down her face. He dumped their glasses and reached for her hand. Katie allowed herself to drift into the feel of his touch. His warm hand slid up to her shoulders. His expression questioned and it made her dizzy and powerless. He saw what he longed to see and kissed her, softly at first and then more fiercely.

His kiss touched a chord of desire and need inside. Blood pounded through her veins as she felt his taunt muscles. Her lips parted and welcomed him. He held her tightly and he tasted salty, warm and tempting. Katie wanted his kiss to last forever and she kissed him back.

She heard a soft triumphant 'Yesss' before he wrapped his arms around her tighter.

Katie's hands moved up the strong

muscles of his back to his wide shoulders and the base of his neck. It felt so right to kiss him. His eyes looked dark and hungry as their bodies melted to a single being and the rapid pulse at the side of his neck matched the frantic beating of her heart. His hand pushed some strands of hair behind her ears before he kissed her again, and his weight pushed her backwards until he pinned her beneath him. The pressure of his arousal told her that he wanted her as much as she wanted him.

Cradled by the warm soft sand, his face just inches away, she needed him more than she ever imagined possible. Her breath caught in her lungs. She was breathless, but who needed oxygen at a moment like this? She snuggled against him as their legs intertwined and his hands caressed her. Slowly his hands moved down along the line of her body to her hips. She shivered with desire.

His voice whispered, 'I dreamed, but nothing compares to the real thing. You're everything I want.'

She stared at him before she answered, 'I'm glad.'

Katie's body ached with need. She forgot everything else, and their closeness was like a drug, lulling her into belonging and euphoria. Amongst abandonment, for a second her brain interrupted with disagreeable thoughts. She loved him, but he had a girlfriend, and a reputation. He was cheating on his girlfriend at this moment — with her. She'd forgotten about Sharon because she loved him. Had he staged today, merely for sex? Paul had cheated on her with another woman. Was she that 'other woman' now?

She pushed him. He froze. The pupils of his eyes were dark and dilated.

'Daniel. What about Sharon?'

His voice was hoarse. 'Forget Sharon.'

Katie pushed again and he moved to the side. 'I can't.'

'Oh hell! What a moment to ask about Sharon.' He sat up. 'You have to trust me. I can't explain now.'

'Why not? What's so difficult?'

He replied harshly, 'I don't want to

talk about her today.'

She stumbled to her feet and he followed in an effortless movement. He tried to grab her hands but she stepped out of his reach and shoved her hands behind her back. 'No. Is she your girlfriend, or not?' Her voice shook slightly and she waited.

His face tightened and his answer came through thin lips. 'Yes, at present I guess Sharon is my girlfriend.'

She stared through a vision blurred by unshed tears. 'You don't care that you're double-crossing her?'

He shrugged his shoulders.

'I'm just one of all the others, aren't I?'

'Don't be silly, and don't pretend you don't want me as much as I want you. Or do you play men along and then blame them when the pace gets too hot?'

She spat out the words. 'Know something? You're condescending, misguided and conceited. Just because I think it is wrong for you to cheat, you suggest I'm some kind of floozy.' She shook her head violently. 'You're wrong! I'm paid to run your office; sex was not part of the contract. I got carried away just now and I regret it already.'

He flinched and rubbed the back of his hand across his mouth.

She wanted him more than anyone she'd met before, or anyone she'd ever meet in the future, because she loved him, but today was a mistake.

'Sharon doesn't know we're together, does she?' She waited. He remained tight-lipped and silent. 'I thought perhaps the rumours were exaggerated, but they're not. Sex and a good time, with no strings attached, is all you want.'

He started to say something, then closed his mouth again. His lips were a thin line. He studied her for a moment before he strode off, leaving her standing.

Katie watched him disappear round the next bend. The wind fretted her hair and she felt terribly cold. She wrapped her arms around herself, feeling lost. Katie half-stumbled to some nearby rocks and sat down. Seconds turned into minutes as she stared at the ocean.

When Daniel returned, Katie rubbed the palms of her hands across her cheeks to remove the remains of tears before he was close enough to see them.

The skin was tight across his cheekbones and his words robbed her of any more illusions. 'There's no point in staying, is there?'

Her voice shook slightly. 'No, there isn't. Let's go!'

His lips were a thin line and his eyes looked cold. 'I'll collect the things. Go back to the yacht.' He turned abruptly and went to collect the picnic basket.

Alongside the yacht, Katie grabbed a rope and pulled herself aboard, bruising her hip. She heard Daniel thrashing his way through the water and hurried below deck to change. When she came on deck, Daniel was dressed and in position at the wheel.

'Katie!'

'Daniel, don't bother!'

'I wish I could make you under-stand.'

'I do. That's the trouble, isn't it? Can we go home now?'

He gave in and started the engine.

She looked back towards the island. After a while, she offered to make coffee, but he refused. He withdrew into himself and so did she. She gazed blindly across the water until she heard, 'Naraotoa ahead of us!'

He moored the yacht. She ignored his outstretched hand to help her disembark. She walked in front of him to his car. From behind her haze of disillusionment, she noticed he greeted a couple of people as they passed. At the hotel she got out swiftly, picked up the basket and took a deep breath before saying, 'See you on Monday?'

'Yes.' He tried again. 'Katie.'

She turned and rushed away. He was Sharon's, and she didn't intend to break that relationship. Even though she loved him, she wouldn't end up as an affair on the side. For her, it was all or nothing.

★ ★ ★

In the end, Katie gave up trying to sleep. She went on the balcony. Clasping her knees within her arms, the silky folds of her pyjamas fell softly as she waited for the first light of dawn to paint the day in ever-deepening shades of red and gold. Another wonderful day was breaking.

She didn't understand Daniel even though she loved him. Avoiding other people, she spent hours walking along the beach. She dreaded Monday morning but she'd get through it somehow.

Getting dressed on Monday morning, she felt tense and sick. Could they work efficiently together and pretend Saturday hadn't happened? When she reached reception, she managed to smile at Amos.

'Daniel phoned. He's busy. Send anything urgent to the plantation office.'

'Thanks, Amos.' The knot in her stomach loosened. For almost the first time she was happy that he wasn't coming in.

Daniel phoned later. Katie's throat seized up when she heard him ask briskly, 'Any problems?'

She covered the phone, took a deep breath and concentrated. 'No. Everything's fine. I want to do that costing for new bed linen with the house-keeper.'

'Go ahead. Anything else?'

Grateful that he couldn't see her face, she replied, 'No, nothing special.'

'Okay! You know where I am in an emergency?'

'Yes, of course.'

'Bye.'

'Bye.' Katie replaced the receiver. At least they managed to talk. Did their outing mean nothing to him?

38

Katie arranged to meet Judy for tennis and a chat. They finished their game early; neither of them felt energetic. They sat at a shady table with an iced drink.

'Heard from Jeff?' Katie asked.

'He writes every couple of days if he can. Working and looking for permanent lodgings fills up most of his time.'

'If he writes that regularly, it shows how much he misses you. Does he like the hospital?'

'Um! He seems very happy so far.'

'Good. Heard anything about your job interview?'

'I'm still waiting. I don't want to apply somewhere else but I'll have to soon.' Judy paused. 'I haven't seen you since Daniel's party. Did you enjoy yourself?'

'Yes. Everyone seemed to enjoy themselves.'

'Was Sharon playing hostess?'

'I don't know. When I arrived, most of the people, including Sharon, were already established and enjoying themselves.'

'Their relationship is a bit odd, isn't it?'

'Daniel and Sharon's? In what way?'

'They're not very affectionate. I saw them down by the harbour this morning.'

Katie glanced down and played with her straw. Daniel had told her he was at the plantation office. 'Perhaps they're trying to keep their lives as private as possible.'

'You're probably right. How's the headache? I've got some aspirin in my bag. Need one?'

'Yes, please. It's not getting any better. I don't want to spoil the rest of the day.'

*   *   *

When Daniel came into the office at the end of the week, Katie tried to pretend it was a day like any other. She hadn't forgotten a thing, but there was no point in tormenting herself about something that couldn't be changed.

Daniel greeted her, looked straight ahead, and went to his office. She was still fighting her devils when he returned with a bunch of inquiries.

He glanced at her with a bland expression and immediately directed his attention to the business in hand. For a moment, Katie was relieved when she realized he didn't intend to mention Paradise Lost, but then she began to feel angry and upset that it meant so little to him. She hadn't forgotten a single second, but he chose to ignore it completely. She stared at the computer screen until her thoughts began to calm again. Perhaps it was better that way, but it didn't stop her wanting him. How could she be so stupid and so weak?

She'd thought about admitting that she was as much to blame. She'd known about Sharon. She was just as responsible. She kept quiet. They worked through the queries with neither of them mentioning anything other than work.

Flicking through the letters, Daniel said, 'Sharon is going to look at our booking system to see if she can suggest any improvements.' He went on turning the pages.

Katie hoped she sounded undaunted. She swallowed a lump in her throat and said, 'Fine. When's she coming?'

'Whenever she has time.' He handed her the letter folder. 'So, that's it. Anything else? If not, I'll be on my way.'

'No. There's an estimate for the carpentry work for the end two bungalows, but it can wait.'

'Leave it for now. I'll study it next time round.' He collected his things and she heard him talking to Ben on his way out. She prayed Sharon would come after she'd left the island.

*   *   *

She didn't. She came without warning. Katie saw her in Daniel's car, coming up the drive. She thought briefly about going into hiding, but she wasn't a coward. She presumed Sharon didn't know about that day on Paradise Lost, otherwise she'd have confronted Katie before now.

She heard Sharon's laughter long before Daniel opened the door and stood aside to let her pass. Katie's mouth spread into a stiff smile. Sharon was wearing a mini-length dress in sky blue with a silver chain belt. With her blond hair and pert figure, she provided the perfect foil to Daniel's dark, athletic looks.

Sharon was very relaxed. 'Hi!'

'Hi!' Katie hoped that it sounded friendly.

'Last time we met was at Daniel's party, and before that it was while I was running around on a hot beach.'

Katie nodded. They hadn't met at Daniel's party, but who cared? She asked, 'Like something to drink? I've just made tea, but if you'd like something else — '

'I'd love some juice, but don't go to any trouble.'

'It's no trouble.' Katie got up and vacated her chair. She was glad to leave. When she returned, Sharon was in her chair and Daniel had his arm across its back. Katie felt a lump in her throat. It reminded her of her own beginnings. It was now the picture of things to come.

Katie moved to Daniel's office and busied herself with some lists. She couldn't concentrate, and listened to their bantering voices. They got on well, and Katie was incredibly envious. They whispered occasionally, so she closed the connecting door. Lesperon phoned and asked her to come to the kitchen. One of the ovens was malfunctioning.

Katie loitered there and then rang a local gas-fitter. She called at the house-keeper's room. When Katie returned to her office, it was empty.

★　★　★

Next day, Daniel handed her a bundle of notes. 'Sharon suggests we should increase our deposit. Compared to the other hotels, ours is pretty low.'

'A larger one might put some visitors off.'

'Yes, I realize all that. Other hotels ask for five percent. I thought three or four would be okay for us.'

Katie nodded. It shouldn't bother her, but as long as she was manager, she'd act as if she'd be around forever.

'She also made some other suggestions. Take a look. See what you think.'

Katie put the notes on the side of the desk. 'Yes, of course. I'll look later. There's no hurry, is there?'

'No. Sharon's suggestions work well in her hotel.'

She nodded silently and worried her lips. She still had difficulty looking at him and forgetting that she loved him. Clearing her throat, she said, 'There isn't much for you today. The cheque for the plumber is on your desk. We have enough cash reserves. The fitter is coming to repair one of the ovens this morning. Lesperon is playing up, and acting like as if we expect him to cook over a campfire. I asked the fitter to give us priority.'

'You don't like Sharon, do you?'

She coloured. 'I don't know her very well. Does it matter what I think?'

'No, of course not. I'm just interested, that's all.'

She flushed. 'I hope I wasn't unfriendly when she was here? That wasn't my intention.'

'No, you're always very polite, even to complete strangers who cause hell. Good! If there's nothing else, let's check those estimates for the paintwork on the two end units. Got them handy?'

'Yes, I'll get them.'

39

Katie met Laura for a cup of coffee in Varua.

'People keep asking me about Daniel and Sharon,' Laura said. 'As if I know what's going on! Everyone thinks Daniel's been trapped at last. Apparently Sharon hasn't even denied suggestions that there's an engagement in the air.'

Katie gripped her cup tighter and concentrated on Laura's voice. 'Really?'

'I'm afraid to ask Daniel myself; he'd bite my head off. Have you heard anything?'

'No. He's not likely to tell me if he hasn't told you and David, is he?'

★ ★ ★

Katie's personal shopping went by the board. She hopped on the bus when it came along. Laura's words still hammered in her brain. She'd adjusted to the fact that Daniel and Sharon were a pair, but her thoughts hadn't gone further. The idea of an engagement made her ache with jealousy. It looked like Sharon was heading for a happy end with the man she loved.

Even a phone call from Colin inviting her out for a drink didn't help much. She played with her glass and eyed him across the table. The bar was one of the less popular ones on the island. Its dim lighting and strange clientele did nothing to improve her mood. Colin kept up a stream of cheerful, meaningless banter. As far as she knew, Colin was always honest with her, even if she disapproved of his lifestyle.

He'd never asked her back to his home, although he probably hoped she'd end up between his sheets one day. He never pushed for more than a fleeting kiss either. She wondered why he didn't stop asking her out.

He cradled an ice-cold beer and told her about his latest plans. Katie listened and nodded in the right places. Telling him that he couldn't afford to do any of those things was a pointless occupation. Katie had given up trying to reform his attitude to money.

If Colin noticed she wasn't concentrating, he didn't say so. Katie felt sorry for him. Something in the past had gone haywire and turned him into a wavering character. Before she got out of the car, Katie leaned across and kissed him on his cheek.

'Thanks, Colin.'

He grinned. 'Night sweetheart. Take care. See you soon.' Katie watched him speed off down the drive.

★ ★ ★

Next morning, Daniel phoned as soon as she reached the office. 'I'm not coming in today. Anything special?'

'No. Can I give the printers the go-ahead?'

'Yes. Anything else?' He sounded preoccupied.

'No, nothing that can't wait.'

'Good. Till tomorrow, or the day after, then.'

* * *

Judy phoned and sounded exuberant. 'Katie, I've got the job.'

'That's great. I'm really pleased for you. When are you leaving?'

'I've just heard I can leave next week. I've booked my flight. I'm not having a farewell party, but I'd like us to meet up for a meal. How about this evening?'

'Yes, I'd like that! The usual place?'

'Yes. Round about seven?'

Katie would miss her. She comforted herself with the thought that she'd be leaving herself soon. She needed to think about her own future. She'd love to continue as a hotel manager, but she probably needed a professional qualification in the UK. How much did a training course cost? She'd check tomorrow for more information.

40

Katie arrived early. She looked around and noticed lots of movement and loud activity down by the harbour. Police cars with blue flashing lights were blocking the entrance. People were racing around and shouting. Suddenly a speed-boat streaked away. There were agitated silhouettes of spectators on the jetty, pointing and shouting. A second speed-boat from the NZ navy pursued it with sirens howling, white seawater frothing in its wake. Katie watched them race parallel to the shore until they disap-peared beyond the next headland.

When Judy arrived, they watched together. People still milled around on the wharf and police were everywhere. Naraotoa only had three policemen and one senior officer, but there were a lot more police this evening. Where'd they come from? The restaurant staff and others were watching too.

The harbour area quietened eventually. Two police cars with sirens blaring and lights flashing drove past and headed towards the main road. The excitement died and everyone went inside.

Katie and Judy chose a quiet corner table. 'Gosh! What a palaver,' Judy commented.

Katie shrugged. 'I'm sure we'll hear all about it tomorrow. No one needs a newspaper in Naraotoa.'

Judy nodded. She began to tell Katie her latest news. As she chattered, Katie envied her a little. Judy's life was on course.

Looking out of the window, Katie was amazed to see Colin hurrying up the hill. With him was the stranger she'd seen smoking near the corner of the hangar at the airport. Colin had insisted that he didn't know him then. Colin looked around nervously. He spotted her, stopped in his tracks and beckoned. Katie went outside.

He was gasping. 'Katie, I swear I haven't done anything bad. I can't explain now, but please believe me.'

The stranger plucked at Colin's sleeve. Katie didn't like the look of him. Colin offered Katie a feeble smile and rushed off. Very puzzled, Katie went back inside.

Judy asked, 'What's up with Colin?'

She shrugged. 'Your guess is as good as mine. He was too nervous to explain.' She picked up the menu.

Judy looked at her friend and hesitated. 'I know it's none of my business, but I don't understand why you like Colin. He's unreliable and he goes round with a lot of strange individuals. People who know him well say he'll end up in jail one day. Be careful, Katie. You're not in love with him, are you?'

'No, I'm not in love with him. I understand why most people think he's erratic and a fly-by-night, but he'll never change his ways if he never gets the chance. He's always been kind and a friend to me. Don't worry; I'm not blind to his faults.'

Judy nodded. 'Good! I hope he never disappoints you.'

After their meal, they walked back towards the main street. Laura and David's car passed them. The girls waved and it stopped.

Laura leaned across. 'Hello you two. I'm glad to have a chance to say goodbye to you, Judy. The best of luck in your new job and for your future.'

'Thanks. I intended to phone you to say goodbye before I left.'

One returning police car interrupted the conversation; it sped towards the harbour, siren still blasting and lights flashing.

Eyeing it, Katie murmured, 'I wonder what's up? It looks like serious trouble.'

David said, 'They raided the Corner Bar near the jetty this evening. It's been under surveillance for some time. It was a den for drug peddling.'

Katie's brows lifted.

He continued, 'The island has had the usual kind of problems with soft drugs before, but suddenly we had cases of hard drug abuse. One kid nearly died of a heroin overdose recently. The local police involved the NZ police and it came to a head this evening.'

Laura's mouth fell open. 'How do you know all this?'

'The police warned us yesterday to be prepared for serious injuries. Luckily, it seems no one has been badly hurt.'

'Wow!' Judy exclaimed.

'The good thing is that they've caught the local dealers and most of their suppliers too. They'll all spend a long time behind prison bars.' He looked at his watch. 'Laura, we're late.'

Laura turned to Katie. 'Bye! Phone me, Katie. I can't play on Thursday; we'll fix another day okay?'

Katie nodded and the two girls talked about happenings until Katie's taxi arrived.

41

Next day, the whole island buzzed. Katie also heard the appalling news that Colin had been taken in for questioning. She knew he was sometimes reckless, but she couldn't believe he was mixed up with major criminals. She busied herself with work, but thought about what she should do. She'd known him for months. She decided she couldn't ignore him now, when he was in real trouble.

After work, she went to the police station. Her mouth was dry as she went inside. One of the local policemen was on duty. He sat typing at a computer in the outer office.

Katie rushed her question. 'Is Colin Walton here, please? I'd like to see him if possible. My name is Katherine Warring.'

The policeman nodded. 'He asked us to contact you, but we've been too busy. Come this way please.'

Katie followed him. 'Is he under arrest?'

'I can't give you any information. The New Zealand police want to talk to him. He'll be taken to Auckland for questioning tomorrow.' He took her to a small unfriendly room and went to fetch Colin. On his return, he warned them, 'Half an hour! And there's a camera!' He locked the door and left.

Katie was sitting by the table. Colin sat opposite and grabbed her hands. 'Thanks for coming, Katie. You're the only person who has.'

'What do you expect? Are you involved? Don't expect sympathy from me if you are.'

His face mirrored his misery. 'At first, I thought it was a clear-cut business deal when these people lent me money. Then they began to pressure me to let them use my plane. I thought they wanted to smuggle alcohol, or cigarettes. I held them at bay for a while and tried to get money to repay them.

They got impatient and used more threatening methods. Remember the car chase and the plane crash? They were behind them. I grew scared and kept finding excuses not to co-operate. In the end, they took my plane and found another pilot. I knew I was in trouble but I hoped they'd leave once they'd achieved their aims.'

Katie freed her hands and ran one of them through her hair. 'Oh, Colin! You must have realized they intended to blackmail you forevermore. You should've gone to the police. Just hoping they'd leave was stupid.'

'Me, going to the police? Can you imagine the reaction? I've been in minor trouble as long as I can remember. They'd assume I was saving myself by dumping others in the muck. Local people — my friends — are involved. I couldn't grass on them.' He ran a hand down his face. 'I know it was wrong. Even if I get out of this mess, I can't stay on Naraotoa. People here will never forget.'

'Tell the police what you just told

me, and answer all their questions. That's your only chance. Tell them you'll bear witness in court.' She took a deep breath. 'I'll confirm the car episode, and I'm not the only one who saw that man at the airport.'

'Katie, you're great. I already figured I'll have to tell them everything if I have a chance of not going to jail. They're questioning me in Auckland tomorrow. They haven't charged me yet, but that might depend on what I tell them. You're leaving the island soon, aren't you? We won't get another opportunity to say goodbye. I realized a long time ago that you didn't feel more than friendship for me but I kept on hoping. I'll always remember you.'

The key turned in the lock and the door opened. 'Time's up!'

Colin stood up. He gave her a gentle kiss. 'You're the loveliest and best person I know. Take care of yourself, and have a wonderful life, I wish I could be part of it.'

She hugged him. 'Don't give up

hope, Colin. Tell them all you know. When this is over, turn over a new leaf. Promise?'

He nodded. 'I'll try to sort myself out. I'll never forget that you came to see me, when everyone else treated me like a pariah.'

* * *

Katie slept badly. She hadn't done much to help Colin, but she'd shown him she hadn't forgotten him either. She'd done the right thing. He wasn't basically bad, just weak.

* * *

Daniel marched over to the window next morning. Before he picked up his mail, he said, 'Heard all about the police raid the day before yesterday?'

'Yes, who hasn't?'

He turned to look out of the window. 'I also heard that you visited Colin yesterday.'

Ruffled, she replied, 'Yes. Is there a law against that?'

'No, of course not, but he's not very popular at present.'

'I know.'

He turned abruptly. His face looked stony. 'Are you in love with him? Is that why you went?'

'Pardon?' The colour flooded her cheeks. 'It's none of your business. I know that you don't like him, Daniel, but Colin was my friend and we spent quite a lot of time together. He told me he had nothing directly to do with transporting or peddling the drugs. He borrowed money off those people, and they had him on a hook. They then pressured him and he turned a blind eye. They found a replacement pilot and used his plane. He acted wrongly. He realizes that himself. I wanted him to know he wasn't completely forgotten. Everyone is innocent until he's proven guilty and I hope Colin can prove that he's guilty of foolishness, but innocent of criminal conduct.'

The muscles on Daniel's jaw moved. He didn't comment. Filling his mug, he grabbed his letters and went into his office. He was in a hurry to get away later on. He packed the unfinished work into his briefcase and left.

Katie told herself she didn't care what he thought. Her last weeks on Naraotoa might be a bit like walking on glass, but she'd manage.

She wondered if people might give her the cold shoulder because she'd visited Colin in jail. People she knew didn't. When the dust settled, some of them even said they admired her courage for not condemning him outright.

She wondered if she'd ever hear from Colin again. She only had his Naraotoa address. If he didn't write before she left, their contact would end. She hadn't yet decided if that was a good thing.

★　★　★

Daniel seemed happier and more relaxed these days. Katie wondered if he'd ever given a single thought to their trip to Paradise Lost. As the days passed, she regretted that she'd gone with him more and more, because it evidently meant nothing to him and that made her feel cheap.

The following week, after they'd cleared the work, he announced, 'It's quiet here, and everything else is functioning well, I'm going to visit my mother. Get me a ticket for next week's flight and for the return flight a week later.'

★ ★ ★

Judy left on Thursday and Katie went to the airport to see her off. They promised to keep in touch. On her way back, staring out of the taxi at the blue ocean flashing by, Katie mused that her ties to the island were unravelling fast. Jeff, Judy and Colin had all left. Soon she'd go too. She'd miss the island like crazy. She couldn't bear to think how much she'd miss Daniel.

42

Katie knew she could manage without Daniel for a while, and he knew so too.

He stunned her, though, when he announced one morning, 'You can have my car while I'm away.'

'You don't have any misgivings? I might drive it into the ditch.'

He gave her a lopsided smile and Katie's heart bumped too fast. 'If I thought you couldn't cope, I wouldn't offer. I usually leave it at David's, but if you take me to the airport and pick me up, you can have it.' As an afterthought, he added, 'When I return, we'll talk about your contract.'

For Katie there was no point. She was leaving.

★ ★ ★

On Thursday she took him to the airport. He looked good. His tanned skin made his shirt seemed brilliantly white. Sitting close to him wasn't easy; it was more straightforward when there was a desk between them.

'My mother lives near Queenstown. The details are in my desk diary. I hope I won't hear from you unless something horrendous happens.' He added, 'You'd like Queenstown. It's a pretty place. Lots of great ski runs nearby.'

Since she couldn't ski, and wasn't ever likely to see Queenstown, Katie didn't comment. They arrived in plenty of time and he parked in front of the departure building. Daniel grabbed his bags and handed her the keys.

'See you next week,' he said. 'Solve things as you see fit.' He smiled. 'Don't wait! You're in charge. Who knows what's happened since we left. Off you go.' He touched his forehead and strolled away.

She was on the way before she remembered about checking the latest exchange rates. She turned around and parked outside the airport buildings again. She noted the rates listed in the small bureau de change in the lobby and went back to the car.

Walking along the perimeter fence, she saw the passengers boarding the plane. She spotted Daniel's tall figure straight away and Sharon's, just one step behind. Katie ceased to function and ice gripped her insides. The vision of them together shouldn't surprise her, but it did. She felt tears gathering. Were they going to see Daniel's mother together? Katie got into the car with her thoughts in chaos. She stared ahead and mused that he'd known they were travelling together; that was why he'd given Katie his car.

She watched the plane take off. It disappeared into an azure sky.

She got on with her work, but she thought non-stop about a solution to her dilemma. She needed one fast, before Daniel and Sharon returned.

43

If Katie stayed until her contract officially finished, it'd be very difficult. Daniel might want to install Sharon in her place. If she was still there when he did, it'd be hell.

She'd never had a day off, although she was entitled to fourteen days. She'd planned to laze for the last fortnight. If she got the work up to date, and left early, she'd cover the remaining discrepancy in days by buying her own ticket. Daniel might even be grateful to establish Sharon without having her around.

The more Katie thought about it, the more convinced she was that it was a perfect solution. She already missed Daniel, and longed to see him again before she left, but her brain told her it was time to go. Her heart ached with all the impossible dreams she kept hidden, but she felt relieved. She'd sort out her heartaches when she was back on the other side of the world.

She had to tell Laura. She was the only close friend she had left. Katie phoned her one afternoon. David had stand-by duty so Katie asked if she was at home. She drove there, hoping Laura would listen without probing or asking too many questions.

They sat on the veranda, looking down towards the harbour. Laura noticed that Katie was very pale and looked unwell. 'What's wrong? You don't look too good. Monthly curse?'

Glad to get started, Katie began, 'No'.

'Not worried about Colin, I hope? He went too far this time. Don't tell me that you're in love with him?'

'Good heavens, no. You're not the first person who's asked me that. We liked each other and he made me laugh. I was grateful for his friendship, even if his contacts were weird.'

'I heard that you visited him in jail. He ought to be grateful for that. I don't think anyone else did.' Her voice was full of disapproval. 'No one forced him to mix with the wrong people. I don't feel sorry for him and neither should you.' She examined Katie's face again. 'There's something else though, isn't there? Out with it! What's the matter?'

Katie had never found it easy to show her feelings, but Laura was a replacement older sister. 'I'm leaving next week.'

Laura looked slightly stunned. 'You're what? Leaving! Daniel's still away, isn't he?'

'My contract ends in three weeks. He owes me vacation time and I'll cover the rest by paying for my own ticket home.'

'Does Daniel know you're going?'

She shook her head.

Laura's brows lifted. 'What's wrong? Can I help?' Laura waited. 'Come on Katie. Trust me. Did you have a row with Daniel before he left? You've learned how to cope with him by now, haven't you?'

'I took him to the airport. I saw Sharon getting on the same plane.' She looked down at her hands. 'I think they'll return engaged or even married. I don't want to be here if that happens.'

Laura studied her face for a moment and drew a breath. 'You've fallen for him? You're in love with Daniel?'

Katie continued to study her hands.

Laura looked concerned. 'I noticed how you chatted about Jeff, or Colin, or anyone else you met, and that you hardly mentioned Daniel. I did think that was strange, but as long as you never said you liked him I didn't worry. I pushed it to the back of my mind after he began partnering Sharon.'

Katie shifted in her chair and met Laura's glance with difficulty.

Laura continued, 'I always wanted Daniel to end up with someone nice, someone like you. I was surprised when he paired off with Sharon. They don't suit. I thought it would just be another of his passing affairs.'

Katie shrugged. 'Sharon is his kind of

woman. He listens to her. He never listens to me — well, not very often!'

'That's not true. I can't remember how often you told me you'd been able to change his mind about something.'

She tried to give a shaky smile. 'Only business decisions. I've never tried to change his private attitude to anything. Once he makes up his mind, he usually sticks to it. I've seen how Sharon is able to influence him. I know you warned me off him, and I kept my distance, but you can't always control emotions, can you?'

'Perhaps it's all tittle-tattle? Daniel has never admitted he was serious about Sharon, or have you heard differently? They act very off-hand with each other and they spend more time in other people's company than together. People in love do things the other way round.'

Katie fixed her eyes on the pattern of her skirt. 'They're both on view publicly all day. It's easy to imagine they enjoy spending private time at his bungalow.

They're alone there whenever they like, as often as they like. Not every pair shows their loving affection.'

Laura said determinedly, 'When someone's in love, you can tell by the way they look, by gestures, and how they act — especially in the beginning. Do you love him, Katie?'

'Yes, I do. But don't ever tell anyone else, not even David. I wanted you to understand why I'm leaving. You've been a great friend to me.'

'Wait until he returns! Make up a cock-and-bull story about a family crisis. Daniel won't like it if you just disappear. You'll leave him with a bad memory if you go without his blessing.'

Katie's eyes misted. 'It doesn't matter what he thinks about me after I'm gone, does it? I coped till now but I wouldn't if he danced attendance on Sharon when I was around. He might notice how jealous I am.' Katie anticipated Laura's next words. 'No, please don't suggest anything else. I know that I'm being a coward, but my mind's made up. Daniel won't give me a second thought once I've gone.'

Laura saw tears trickling down Katie's cheeks. 'I'm so sorry, Katie. I wish I could put things right. I wish I'd warned you more often. I thought you were safe because you were chalk and cheese. He's impulsive and dynamic, and you're good-natured and calm. I don't think Sharon will make him happy.' She got up and hugged Katie. 'When are you planning to leave?'

Katie's voice sounded stronger. 'He's returning on Thursday. I'm leaving on the same plane. I've booked a non-stop flight from Auckland to Heathrow on Saturday morning.'

'I still wish that you'd wait and talk it over with him. You don't need to tell him the whole truth. It'd be enough to explain that you think it's better that you are out of the way when Sharon takes over.'

She shook her head. 'It'll make no difference in the long run.'

'I'll miss you. You'll keep in touch?'

'Yes, of course. I want you and David to visit me one day.'

Laura handed her some tissues and went to get them something to drink. It gave Katie time to adjust again.

* * *

Daniel phoned. Ben took the message. He confirmed that he'd be back on Thursday. Katie brought everything up to date. He might have a backlog elsewhere, but there wasn't one at Rockley.

After work, she took numerous pictures of the island, even parts she'd never visited before. She drove to Daniel's bungalow one day. When she stepped out onto the carport's cement floor, shrivelling blossoms from hibiscus bushes blew round her sandals. She remembered the night of the party, how he'd shown her around the bungalow and how she spent Christmas day with him. Katie sat outside his bedroom and picked a large red hibiscus flower from a bush growing at the side, as a souvenir. She sat contentedly for a while looking at a panorama he'd see for the rest of his life. She only had one photo of him. Taken that day on Paradise Lost.

★   ★   ★

On Wednesday evening, she cornered Ben. 'Ben, I won't be here tomorrow.'

'What do you mean?' He paused. 'Oh, yes. You're picking Daniel up from the airport.'

'Daniel's coming and I'll be leaving — on the same plane.'

He looked shocked. 'What? Does Daniel know?'

She shook her head. 'It's time for me to go.'

'He'll be mighty angry. Is there something wrong at home? Can I help?'

'No, everything is all right. My contract is finishing and I'm leaving. The hotel is running well.'

'Without saying goodbye? Wait! Give him a chance.'

Katie was unable to say any more; she'd give herself away. She reached up and hugged Ben's huge frame. Her eyes glistened. 'Don't worry, there's nothing wrong. Daniel will understand. Thanks for being a rock in the storm. I'll never forget you. Please say goodbye to Sarah and everyone in the village.'

She turned and walked away, leaving Ben baffled.

44

Katie hoped her letter gave nothing away.

Dear Daniel,

As you see, I'm not here to greet you personally. I hope you'll not be too angry when you find I've gone home.

Everything is up to date and I've prepared as much as I can in advance, so I hope I you won't have too many headaches. With your help, I'm sure Sharon will grasp everything much quicker than I did.

Everything is on your desk, or in the safe (I've left the keys in reception).

My vacation time and paying my own fare will recompense you for the time I should have stayed until my contract ended officially. I hope you'll

319

agree that we're quits.

I wish you happiness. I'll never forget Naraotoa; it was a dream come true.

Look after yourself, and yours.
— Katie

She put it in an envelope and addressed it to Daniel.

* ★ ★ ★

Next morning her suitcases were already in Daniel's car when she went for a last solitary walk along the empty beach. On her return, a knock on the door revealed Ben with a brown paper package in his hands. 'Sarah asked me to give you this and to wish you God speed.'

Katie opened the package and found a colourful sarong and a matching top. She felt the tears rolling down her cheeks. She'd never wear it. She'd keep it in some drawer to remind her of some generous and kind people on the other side of the world.

'Thank her, Ben, and give her a kiss from me. She's so kind. I'll write, I promise!' She shoved the keys into his hands. 'I was going to leave them at the desk, but you take them until Daniel gets back.'

She picked up the rest of her things and fled without a backward glance. She scurried along the outside of the building to avoid meeting anyone. Driving carefully, she reached Laura's bungalow in plenty of time. Laura was waiting. When she got in and fastened the belt, Katie gave her the letter for Daniel.

'I've explained as best I could. I hate goodbyes, so please don't wait at the airport. Drive straight home again.'

Laura patted her hand and wished she could stop her, but Katie was too determined.

Outside departures, Katie loaded a trolley with her luggage. She made an effort to be calm. 'Please give my love to David. I'll write when I'm home.

Thanks for being my friend, Laura. Look after yourself and your family. God Bless!' Katie kissed her on the cheek with some tears escaping again, before she turned away. She didn't look back and went through the sliding doors.

Katie asked the information desk to page Daniel when the plane landed and tell him his car was at Laura's. She waited for the departure announcement in the furthest corner of the small room. The plane landed and emptied its passengers, although Katie didn't see them.

It left on time with Katie as one of its passengers. She looked down at Naraotoa. Somewhere far below were all the places and people she'd grown to love. Perhaps Daniel would be angry, but the hotel was functioning like clockwork. He'd have no cause to complain. She kept her face towards the window so that the man in the next seat wouldn't see she was crying.

45

Daniel took a taxi to David's. His car was alongside the steps. He threw his bags onto the back seat and bounded up the stairs.

Laura took a deep breath. This wasn't going to be easy. 'Hello, Daniel. Had a good trip?'

'Hi! Yes, fine.' He looked around. 'Where's Katie? She was supposed to pick me up. Is something wrong? Is she ill?'

'Katie's left. She gave me a letter for you.'

'What do you mean, she's left? Where's she gone?'

'Back to the UK. She flew out in the same plane you came in on.' She saw the shock in his face. The devil-may-care look vanished in a flash. He looked stunned.

'Is there a family crisis?'

Laura shook her head. She handed

him Katie's letter and the car keys. 'I'll get you something to drink. Back in a minute.' She went inside.

He slit the flap and read Katie's words.

Laura came back with fruit juice. She put it on the table. He was standing at the rail. Katie's letter hung loosely in his hand. He turned suddenly and shook the paper like an angry dog. 'What's this about?'

'I don't know. May I read it, or is it very personal?'

He looked at her with blank eyes. The bubble of anger burst. He handed her the letter wordlessly. She glanced through it quickly and handed it back.

'Is this a joke?'

'Oh no, Daniel. Far from a joke. I took her to catch the plane. I saw her leave.'

'What in God's name has happened? When I went, everything was all right. What's upset her so much that she rushes off without any kind of warning?'

Laura gestured. 'I tried to make her wait. Katie just couldn't bear to stay any longer. Know why? You. Or to be more precise, you and Sharon.'

'Would you please explain? I haven't upset Katie for ages, as far as I know, and what has it to do with Sharon?'

Laura must tread carefully; she'd promised Katie. She wouldn't tell all, but Daniel wanted an explanation. He'd always managed to hide his feelings, but at this moment, he was a shocked man. He sat down and waited.

'When you left, Katie saw Sharon getting on the same plane. She recalled the rumours about an impending engagement. In fact, I'd even mentioned it to Katie myself because I thought she should know.'

Looking puzzled, he asked, 'What are you talking about? An engagement? Whose engagement?'

'Yours. Yours and Sharon's. Don't ask me who started it. It has nothing to do with me. When people asked Sharon, she left them guessing and it fed fuel to the flames. Katie saw you two getting on the plane and decided the rumours were true.' Laura noted that he was breathing deeply. She ignored the danger signs.

Daniel uttered through thin lips, 'Gossip from start to finish. It's incredible that people haven't anything better to do with their time.'

Laura ignored him. 'Don't sit there and pretend otherwise. You've been going out with Sharon for months. We all wondered what was going on. How serious you were.'

'What has this to do with Katie leaving? I still don't understand.'

Laura snapped, 'Don't you? Use your imagination! Before she came here, a boyfriend cheated on her. She made friends with Colin, Jeff, the others, and me, because she needed friendship. She came as a stranger to a strange environment and your initial meeting probably torpedoed any idea of you and friendship. She tried to ignore you. Later you were tied to another woman.'

She paused and they stared at one another. She held his gaze.

'If you mean what I'm thinking, I

only wish everyone minded their own business. I go away and come back to chaos caused by other people. I never considered getting engaged to Sharon. We were never more than friends.'

'Then for God's sake, why didn't you tell people that?'

'I couldn't! Just for your information, Sharon is getting married soon to Gareth, the chap who visited Christmas-time. He wasn't her cousin.' He gazed into the garden. 'Do you know when she's flying? Which airline?'

'She mentioned Air New Zealand. I remember her saying it was a non-stop flight from Auckland on Saturday.'

His voice was coloured with hope. 'She's in Auckland until Saturday? David had a timetable when you organized Ian's last flight. Still got it?'

Laura bit her lip. 'In case you've forgotten, the first scheduled flight is next Thursday.'

'There are private planes, a helicopter service, or even ships, if everything else fails.'

She stared, nodded, and rushed off to search through the muddle on David's desk. She felt like hooting. He was going after her. Even Daniel wouldn't drag her back just to finish her contract. She pounced on the brochure and hurried back to hand it to him wordlessly.

Impatiently, he thumbed the pages. 'Here it is. Flight 458, Saturday, 11.35 am. I'm off. I have to sort things out before I leave. I'll check if Willie Parsons can fly me. He'll do anything if you give him enough money.'

'Need help at the hotel? I'm no use in the office, but I can cope with irate guests and Lesperon's tantrums.'

He tried to look amused; the first untroubled expression she'd seen on his face since he arrived. 'You're more likely to start a revolution, but if you could manage the bank business for me that would be a great help.'

She nodded.

'I'll call later to explain and I'll talk to David then.'

She caught hold of his sleeve. 'Daniel, bring her back. She wanted to stay. She just couldn't face the idea of you and Sharon together.'

He'd never sounded more serious. 'You can bet I'll do my damnedest.'

46

Daniel stared into space for several seconds before he started the engine. He drove to the airport and arranged to fly with Willie Parsons next morning.

On the road again, he tried to concentrate on work. From Katie's letter, he guessed she'd organised her work. The staff would keep the hotel running. If Laura acted as go-between for the bank, everything should tick over until they came back.

He refused to consider the possibility that Katie wouldn't come back. He focused on present problems. The plantation would be okay for a while, but he needed to sort out the payroll. He couldn't expect the workers to wait for their money. The other businesses ran under partnerships. He only needed to phone around and tell them he'd be away a while longer.

When he walked into the lobby, Ben's expression told him there was no need for explanations. For once, the lobby was empty.

Ben came gave him no greeting. 'I tried to make her wait. She wouldn't listen.'

He nodded. 'I know. She's very determined. It's one reason I like her.'

'I don't know why she left, but I can guess. She was mighty upset when you went missing in that storm and after that I put two and two together.'

Daniel wore a deadpan face but then the mask slipped. Ben knew him too well. 'I wish I'd noticed that. I thought I had time.'

'The workers like her and you know how sparing they are with their approval.'

'She's in Auckland until Saturday. Do you think the hotel can tick over for a while without us? I'll ask Mrs. Stannard to handle the bank.'

Ben beamed. 'We'll manage.'

'Told anyone else about Katie leaving?'

'No, I decided to wait. I told anyone who asked that she had a day off.'

'Good man! Tell them she's on vacation. I'll check the office now and authorise this month's wages. Give me the key to the safe. You'll get it back before I leave. When I finish here, I'll go to the plantation.'

'I'll be here until six, officially, but I'll stay as long and as often as necessary to keep things functioning. Don't worry about the hotel.'

★ ★ ★

Katie's office felt very empty. She'd cleared out all the drawers as if she'd never existed. Only a slender vase with sprigs of pink frangipani stood on top of the filing cabinet. The room was tidy; she was a methodical worker. It looked the same as the day she'd arrived. There was one difference though. He'd changed.

As he suspected, she'd left anything that needed his attention in tidy bundles on his desk. Labelled with brief explanations, it took little effort on his part to complete what she'd begun. After dealing with that, he picked up the details for the wages for the bank and pushed them into a folder to take with him. He gave the signed letters to Ben to post.

Daniel spent the rest of the day at the plantation office. There'd been no pressing problem in his absence apart from a broken truck. It was already at the local repair shop. That afternoon he sorted out the plantation payroll for the month. He'd drop the details off at the bank and organize the proxy for Laura on his way to the airport tomorrow.

He phoned Laura to put her in the picture, and then she transferred his call to David's study. At first, neither of them mentioned Katie. David asked about the skiing, and then told Daniel some news about the sailing club.

Finally, David said quietly, 'Laura told me about your plans. If Katie is just another girl for an affair, please forget it. I know I've no right to interfere, but I like Katie and you'll hurt her unless she means more to you than that. Don't bulldoze her; give her a chance to breathe and react. To all appearances, Katie is very self-assured, but she's very vulnerable underneath.'

* * *

Close to midnight, Daniel felt mentally exhausted. There was some basic foodstuff in the fridge, thanks to Muriel. He made himself some sandwiches and took them, and a bottle of beer, out onto the veranda to stare blindly at the black and silver lights blinking on the surface of the ocean.

He flew out with Willie Parsons next morning.

* * *

In Auckland, he went straight to one of the desk clerks. He felt almost physical relief when the man looked up and nodded silently. Katie's flight was non-stop. If he couldn't persuade her to stay here, he'd buy a ticket and go with her. He'd then have twenty-six hours to talk her round.

Searching for her was pointless. He booked into an airport hotel. He just wanted a chance to explain everything. He didn't blame her for not trusting him; she assumed the worst because he'd hidden the facts. That trip to Paradise Lost showed him she wasn't indifferent; now it was up to him to convince her by telling her the truth. He couldn't imagine life without her anymore and hoped it wasn't too late.

47

Katie reclaimed her large suitcases from the lockers. She was early, and decided to go to a nearby bistro. She didn't expect to see anyone, so she paid no attention to other people. She chose a seat near the window with a view of the runway. She couldn't believe it when she saw Daniel's familiar figure winding its way through the tables towards her.

Her mind stopped working and she stared at him, lips parted, in utter surprise. Finally, she asked, 'What are you doing here? Why aren't you on Naraotoa?' She stood up. A paperback slipped to the floor. She looked at his lean features and felt pure happiness for a moment. Perhaps he was in one of his arrogant, pushy moods and had come to make a fuss about her breaking her contract.

'Funny, I wanted to ask you the same

question. Why aren't you on Naraotoa working for me like old billy-oh?'

Her mouth felt dry. She sat down again. She needed something solid to support her trembling knees. 'Didn't you get my letter? I left it with Laura.'

'Yes, I got it.' He folded his long frame into the opposite chair.

She tried to shove her hands under the table. Daniel grabbed them and held them tight. She tried to free them but his grip tightened. She hoped the storm inside her would subside fast. It didn't. She wanted to look blasé, but floundered badly. She looked down instead; her brain was in turmoil. She couldn't avoid his glance forever. It wasn't difficult for her to guess he'd come for a good reason. She'd have to listen, whether she wanted to or not.

'Let's sort one thing. I'm not engaged to Sharon. I never considered getting engaged to her, not for a single moment. She's an intelligent, attractive woman, but we didn't have an affair. I realize everyone, including you, assumed so.

We intended it to look that way. I'll explain about Sharon in a moment, but I swear she was never my girlfriend. Do you believe me?'

She gazed at him, and after a moment, she nodded.

'Good! Laura and Ben both think you disappeared for personal reasons.'

Her throat was knotted, but he wanted a comment so she gathered some coherent thoughts from somewhere and managed to stutter, 'I went because I thought it was best for you, me and the hotel.'

'Really? Laura suggested it had something to do with the rumours about my engagement.'

Katie tried desperately to sound nonchalant. 'Sharon was your girlfriend and I presumed she would take over when I left. She'd already checked our system. My contract was almost finished so I figured my leaving early would make the takeover easier.' Katie noticed his frown. She threw back her head and struggled on. 'Sharon is a trained hotelier and after running Rockley for some months on my own, I wasn't sure if we would work together without conflicts developing.'

'Sharon isn't a trained hotelier.'

Katie was baffled. 'She isn't?'

'You're too conscientious to leave without formally signing everything over. That's how you function. What was the real reason?'

Katie glued her attention on the single carnation in the centre of the table. She tried to ignore his question and remained silent.

'I wish you'd be honest with me. You made me extremely miserable.'

She hesitated, blinking. 'Miserable? What about?'

'Can't you guess? Must I spell it out?'

Her head shot up. 'If you followed me, I'm sure you'll tell me, whether I want to hear or not. You'd hardly fly to New Zealand, after you'd just flown from New Zealand, without a damned good reason.'

The corners of his mouth curved. He

considered her in silence and then said, 'Katie, when you left, I lost the only thing I love more than any possession, or any of my friends. I want you back for selfish reasons. I love you. I've loved you for a long time. I want to share your life with you, if you'll let me.'

A faint flush flooded her cheeks. 'Please don't joke about something so serious.'

'Who's joking? I've never been more serious in the whole of my life. I hope I'm doing this right because I'll never do it again. I'll do anything to convince you.'

The world stood still. Katie struggled and finally managed, 'Honestly?' She studied his expression and saw the truth.

He squeezed her hand. 'By everything that's holy, I swear that I love you, Katie. I'm sure that I always will. I want you with me on Naraotoa'

She caught her breath. Slowly, a feeling of utter contentment spread through her and she knew why she was alive. 'I'm so glad that you never lie, and are so outspoken.'

The air fizzled between them. Her words and her eyes told him what he wanted to know.

Katie had nothing to lose anymore. 'Yes, I left because I love you. I couldn't face seeing you and Sharon sharing a future together. My contract had almost ended anyway, so I decided that Sharon would be able to step straight into my shoes.'

'Sharon isn't big enough to step into your shoes; no one is. You're irreplaceable. It was a coincidence that Sharon and I were on the same flight. I didn't know she was leaving until I met her in the departure lounge. I've longed to tell you the truth. I almost did once or twice, but stopped because I'd promised to keep my mouth shut. Do you believe me?'

Katie sighed quietly. 'Yes, I believe you.'

He enfolded her in his arms and kissed her hungrily. They were mouth on mouth and body to body; two people as one. He took her face between his hands and kissed her slowly again. They stared silently at each other, safe in the knowledge that they had all the time in the world. Daniel tucked a strand of her hair behind one ear. 'You can't imagine how much I want you. I longed to tell you I cared, but I couldn't. I was sworn to secrecy.'

She waited expectantly.

He pulled her chair across and they sat down. He took her hands again. 'Promise not to repeat what I'm about to tell you.'

Katie nodded. 'Of course, but why all the secrecy?'

'Remember the drug ring the police ripped apart on Naraotoa not long ago?'

'Yes. Has this something to do with Colin? I swear I didn't know about his involvement. Those criminals tricked him into passive participation.'

He viewed her with indulgence. 'When you befriend someone, you go all the way, don't you? I should be jealous, but you just said you loved me, so I'll be generous. Don't expect me to change my opinion about him. He doesn't deserve your friendship.'

'I'd never knowingly be involved with anyone who messed around with drugs. Colin has a laid-back attitude about lots of things and I tried to make him see sense.'

He brushed her words aside. 'I tried to warn you, but stubborn as you are, you just thought I was interfering in your personal life. I was intensely jealous but I couldn't explain why. That near plane crash gave me the biggest shock of my life because I knew all about the drug cartel by then, and Colin was already under observation. I was out of my mind with concern that day.'

Katie decided this wasn't the right moment to mention the car chase. She could imagine his reaction when he heard about that. She listened instead.

'Sharon is a police woman.'

Katie's eyes widened. 'A police woman?'

He nodded. 'She's a detective in the NZ narcotics department. They needed names, places, contacts, routes on Naraotoa. The bosses of the drug cartels are experts in covering their tracks. The small fish are easy to trace. The further up the pyramid you go, the harder it gets. At first, the police tried getting information via the locals. It didn't work and one of the policemen was even shot in the process. A former pal of mine works in Sharon's department and asked me if I'd help. Sharon came to work undercover. The island's police were familiar to everyone, but Sharon wasn't. Sharon needed a believable cover-up to move around without evoking suspicion. My friend asked me to give her that cover. I wanted to keep these parasites off the island as much as the police did. I didn't mind people thinking Sharon and I were a twosome — until I realized I was in love with you. They thought it would take a couple of weeks, but it turned into months.'

'What did you have to do?'

'Not much. Sharon was my sham girlfriend, so she had a first-class, plausible cover. She collected information at get-togethers, in restaurants, clubs and the like. Together we sorted out possible transport routes, hiding places, and contacts on the island. We expected them to use boats in the beginning, but they shifted to planes. They needed a gullible plane owner. Colin had financial problems, so they lent him money, and then they pressured him into co-operating. You know the rest.' He paused. 'I can't say when I fell in love with you; it just happened. I was extremely jealous of Jeff, or Colin, or anyone else who filled your leisure time, but I daren't show it.'

Katie touched his cheek. 'I tried to ignore you too. It got harder as time went on. I didn't want you just for one day, like the one we spent together on Paradise Lost.'

He lifted her hand, kissed her fingers and then the inside of her palm. The mere touch of his lips made her feel breathless. 'That day on Paradise Lost was wonderful. It was the weekend before the police struck. I didn't tell Sharon; she'd have stopped me. We were like two sides of the same mirror, until you started thinking sensibly. It was stupid of me to believe you'd forget your principles when I wasn't free to explain. You'll never know how tempted I was, but the showdown wasn't far off so I clung to the hope I'd be able to explain when the police action finished.'

Katie's cheeks glowed. 'I presumed you were double-timing Sharon and playing around with me. You don't have the best of reputations, do you? I thought I was just another potential sex adventure. Afterwards I told myself I was as much to blame. I could have blocked things from the start but I got carried away.'

His eyes twinkled. 'Katie, let's get something straight. These rumours about my love life are wild exaggerations. I've had girlfriends, just as you've

346

had boyfriends. I liked some girls — I wouldn't have gone out with them if I didn't — but I never loved anyone like I love you. You're different. You are wonderfully special, the other half of me that was always missing. I want you with me always. There'll be no reason or rhyme in my life if you go away.'

'Can we go back to Paradise Lost one day?' she asked.

'Can we pick up where we left off?' The blue of his eyes intensified and his mouth formed into an infectious smile. Katie laughed and kissed him quickly. A waitress interrupted them. Daniel ordered champagne. The waitress studied their faces and nodded.

'Why didn't you tell me everything straight after the police left?' Katie prompted.

'I was still sworn to secrecy. The drug bosses still don't know the truth. Sharon and I need to keep our part in the investigation secret. She's already pleaded family worries and won't be coming back to Naraotoa. I went to Auckland to get permission from Sharon's boss to tell you the truth. It took a lot of persuasion. And then I did visit my mother. Oh, by the way, Sharon sent you a letter.' He took an envelope from his jacket and gave it to her. He paused for a second. 'I was panic-stricken when I found you'd gone. I looked forward to telling you the truth at last, and you'd vanished.' His voice lost its light tone. 'I was too tough when you arrived. Then later, when I longed to be with you, I couldn't because of the police work. I'm sorry about the confusion, the misunderstandings, and the mix-ups. I don't deserve you.'

She kissed him. 'You do, because I love you.'

He chortled. 'When I think about our first meeting, it's a wonder you didn't head straight back out the door.'

She tilted her head. 'I actually thought about it, but I wanted to prove you wrong.'

'Thank God for that agency. And thank God that fate was kind to us.'

She smiled and touched his face with her fingertips. He kissed them gently and Katie's pulses galloped again. The waitress returned. Daniel handed Katie a glass of champagne. 'Here's to us. I'll never be cantankerous or secretive with you again, promise! You can twist my arm off if I ever act like a complete idiot again.'

'Will you put that in writing? Actually, I think you've improved since we first met; you haven't been unreasonable for ages.' She lifted her glass. 'To us.'

'You know it's difficult for me to share decision-making, but you're different. I'm offering you a lifetime job. Interested? I happen to know your present contract is ending soon.'

'The wages?'

'A devoted husband, a home, children I hope, and as good a life as I can possibly give you.'

Joy bubbled up and her eyes sparkled. 'That sounds wonderful. By the way, I don't want to change you. I'll take you as you are.'

He whooped. 'I knew it. I've found the perfect woman. Now that we're in New Zealand, let's visit my mum. I've already told her all about you, and she's dying to meet you. We'll persuade your parents and the rest of your family to visit Naraotoa. Perhaps I can persuade you to marry me by then. An island wedding celebration is wonderful. Who knows, you might even get a tivaevae as a present.'

'You move fast, don't you? You don't even know if we're suited yet.'

'We are. I'm positive.' He paused. 'I do understand if you need more time to be sure; even if I'm absolutely certain already.'

'You may change your mind when you know me better.'

'Never! Know why? I don't just love you, Katie; I like you too. We'll be friends, lovers and colleagues. I've never been more certain about anything in my life.'

'I was meant to come to Naraotoa. It was destiny.' She saw his lips twitch.

'Don't you dare laugh at me.'

Tongue in cheek, he gave in. 'All right, believe it if it makes you happy.'

'It might have ended badly, but — ' They heard the announcement for passengers to check in for Heathrow. 'Oh, damn. I'll lose my money.'

'Who cares about money?' He tilted his head. 'Okay, give me your ticket. I'll handle it. Are your parents expecting you?'

'No, they're on holiday. I was going to find a new job before they returned, if I could.'

'You've just got one for life. Managing Rockley, and managing me.'

'Sounds like a wonderful offer. Too good to miss.'

He smiled softly. 'I'll never intentionally hurt you again, Katie. Never. I'll love you eternally instead.'

The way he looked at her made her feel wonderfully happy. Perhaps he'd been a wanderer in the past, but now an unexplainable and magical pull had drawn them together and would tie them firmly through the coming years.

'I don't want more,' she said.

Another announcement about the departure brought them back to earth. He touched her face. 'I'll just sort out your ticket. I know someone on the desk. Back in a minute.' With a backward glance, Daniel sprinted away. Katie watched until he was out of sight. She remembered Sharon's letter and slit the envelope.

Dear Katie,

I hope Daniel has explained. He wanted to tell you everything a long time ago, but I stopped him. I had to protect him, and indirectly you too, by keeping you apart. Daniel's a great guy. Once he gave his word, he put his personal life on slow burn. I saw how hard it was for him to keep up the pretence.

He's never admitted it but I sense that he loves you. I often wished I could have released Daniel from his promise and let you two get to know each other. I hope you'll forgive me. Best wishes — Sharon

Katie folded the letter. Daniel returned and wasted no time. He kissed her again. In a haze of euphoria and knowing he loved her, Katie mused that now it would always be like this.

'Daniel, do you realize that all Naraotoa thinks you're going to marry Sharon? What will people think when you start flaunting me around instead?'

He laughed throatily and kissed her again. 'They'll do what they always do — gossip! This time will be different though. They'll chatter about how serious I am, especially after you move in with me.'

THE END